Poison's Christmas

the apocryphile press
BERKELEY, CA
www.apocryphile.org

apocryphile press
BERKELEY, CA

Apocryphile Press
1700 Shattuck Ave #81
Berkeley, CA 94709
www.apocryphile.org

Printed in the United States of America
ISBN 978-1-937002-94-7

STEVEN L. CASE

Poison's Christmas

A NOVEL

Dedication

This book is dedicated to Becky. I use Embraceable You as my ringtone for her. I keep missing her calls because I get caught up in the daydream of waltzing with her on a beach somewhere. I would waltz with her anywhere, to any song. She made all of my dreams come true.

Special Thanks To...

Aprille and Eric, who listened to all my stories over and over and over.

John Mabry, who somehow managed to get this book out there without grabbing his laptop and repeatedly bashing it against the wall.

Every church I have ever worked for. Remember Jesus said to forgive.

Trader Joes. I mentioned them in the Acknowledgments in my last book in hopes of some free coffee or chocolate...nuthin'... thought I'd give it another shot.

You can download the song performed by Jenny the papergirl at the end of this book by visiting www.stevecasespeaks.net and clicking on *books*. (Double special thanks to Ms Eleanor Baum for writing the music and performing it.)

Prologue

December 24, 1993

There was only one person in the entire world that Marvin allowed to call him Marvin. Most folks called him by his given nickname, which was Tuba. Tuba was a giant—well over six feet tall and broad in the shoulders. These things were exaggerated around this time of year by the heavy coat and scarf that he wore.

If you called Tuba "Marvin," he would smile quietly and then ask you politely to call him "Tuba" just like everybody else. If you did it again, he would put a massive hand on your shoulder and whisper in your ear that he liked to be called "Tuba." He would take your hand, lift it over your shoulder and put it on the floor. That was it — he held your hand and put it on the floor. You, being attached, had no choice but to follow it. More than one person in Melvina's Diner had "kissed the linoleum," as the process had come to be called. Most people just weren't stupid enough to say "Marvin" more than twice.

Tuba drove a truck. He had no family, only a few close friends, and an uncanny ability to drive for long hours. Tuba was also one of the few truckers who didn't mind working holidays. On the dashboard of his truck, he had set up a small Nativity scene that he had purchased at a truck stop in Georgia. He had two CDs of Christmas music: one was Elvis, the other was the Beach Boys. Tuba knew every note and sang along at the top of his lungs. Like his father, he only got out the Christmas music after the first Sunday in Advent, and put it away again on December 26th.

He was going to have to put his Christmas CDs away in two days, and was going to miss them, but he knew that if he listened beyond the 26th he'd get sick of the songs and that was no way to celebrate Jesus' birthday. He sipped his coffee and looked out the window of the diner at the snow as it fell past the light poles in the parking lot. The snow wasn't swirling or drifting down, which meant it was wet, which meant it would freeze, which meant ice. Tuba didn't mind snow and rain and wind, but ice made him cautious. He tried not to show it as he finished his cake in his favorite booth. It was the only booth where he could look out the window, keep an eye on the clock, and watch Irene the waitress as she hurried about behind the counter. Irene was a sweet girl who had been cursed with an old woman's name. Most people called her "Rene."

Tuba loved chocolate cake. He would carefully scrape the whipped cream off the top of the frosting and set it onto the edge of the plate. When the cake was gone, he would push the whipped cream over, work the leftover crumbs into it, and then eat it. He took great care to be sure there were no crumbs in his bushy beard, placed a tip on the table, and stood up.

"It's mean out there," Irene called to him from the cash register.

"I've got vegetables," Tuba said, referring to what was in the truck.

Their conversations were always this short, but Tuba dreamed of scooping her small frame into his arms and whisking her away to an island somewhere. In his dreams they always drove his truck to a secluded island, where they would wear bathing suits at 8:00 in the morning. They would eat fruit for breakfast and stay up late into the night. Irene never told him, but she had the same dream.

He walked to the counter and pulled his wallet out of his pocket. She placed a white paper sack on the counter. "What's that?" he asked.

"Christmas cookies," she said. "I made them myself."

"Rene, you didn't have to," he started.

"Shush," she said, and he shushed.

He handed her the money for his meal. She already knew that there was a 21% tip lying back on his table. (Actually, she was wrong this time. Though he consistently left 21%, this time there was a 50% tip and a Christmas card he had spent half an hour picking out. He had been the largest thing in the Hallmark store, and the tiny elderly woman clerk had followed him around as if he'd been going to bump into one of the racks of ceramic Christmas ornaments.) Irene came around the corner of the counter and began to tie his scarf for him. "Are you sure you want to go out? The weatherman says it's not going to let up."

"Then I'd better get started," he said.

Irene surprised him by pulling on the end of his scarf until his face was down by hers. She kissed him on the cheek just above where his beard started. There were a few other truckers and drivers in the diner, who all went "Oooooooooooo!"

Tuba turned as red as his scarf.

"Merry Christmas," Irene said.

Tuba looked at the floor, said "Merry Christmas," grabbed his white paper sack and hurried out the door into the cold Pennsylvania winter.

Just three exits past the Pennsylvania state line lies the town of Emmelton. Just off the exit is a trucker's nightmare called Shepherd's Pass—so named because most of the truck drivers who attempt it at the wrong time of year find themselves repeating the 23rd Psalm. Shepherd's Pass is a full mile of twisting and turning, with a hard rock wall on one side and on the other...nothing but air.

Tuba was singing along with the Beach Boys' Christmas tape when he became profoundly aware that the brakes, though he was applying them, were not slowing him down in the least. "Well, that's not good at all," he said out loud.

He looked at the baby Jesus in the Nativity on his dashboard. "A little help?" he asked, but the plastic baby did not answer. Tuba forced the wheel to the right, slamming the truck against the side of the mountain. He was no longer concerned about making his destination on time—his primary concern now was stopping.

The side of his metal truck scraped the rock, sounding remarkably like a can opener—a very large can opener—a very large can opener opening a can that was somehow alive and screaming. Tuba heard a tire blow. The rig slid to the left, taking out several wooden posts that held a rusty guardrail. "They needed to replace that anyway," Tuba thought.

He looked again at the Nativity on his dashboard and saw that the baby Jesus had rolled out of his tiny plastic manger. It was probably lying on the floor somewhere. Tuba's headlight picked up a patch of dry road about 30 feet in front of him. He once again applied the brakes with the skill of a lifelong trucker.

The brakes screamed, but Tuba managed not to. The truck stopped in one long slow moment that, in Tuba's mind, lasted at least a year. The cab of the truck went through the guardrail. The front tires tasted midair before the cab slammed down onto the rock. Tuba wondered if he was having a heart attack. He looked out his left window and saw that there was no road beneath him. He wondered if he could get out of the cab, hang onto the side of the truck, and work his way back to solid ground. Inhaling as much air as he could, and slowly letting it pass through his mouth in a long, loud whistle, he put his hand on the door to open it.

At that moment, Tuba became aware of a light in the seat next to him. He turned and saw a man taller than himself sitting there, whose clothes and face were so clean they almost shone. The smell was so pure that Tuba was suddenly filled with memories of clean white sheets, peppermint Lifesavers, and wedding cake frosting. The man in the bright clothes leaned over, picked up the tiny baby Jesus from the floor of the cab, and gently placed it in the tiny manger.

"Thanks." Tuba said.

The man, who was glowing white, smiled. He seemed to get even brighter. He said, "You're most welcome, Marvin."

Tuba said, "Call me Tuba."

The rock beneath the tires cracked loudly. In the next moment, the cab of the truck was pointed straight down at the ground. Tuba heard the sickening sound of the last of his eighteen wheels leaving the road. The man in white raised his arms as if he were on a roller coaster and said, "Whooooooooooo-Hooooooooooooooo!"

Chapter One

Twelve years later....

It was never Poison Davenport's intention to steal Christmas—but once he had it in his garage, he realized the hard part was going to be putting it back.

Poison was seventeen. He was named after the Eighties heavy metal band. Well, they were as heavy metal as you could get in the Eighties and still use that much mousse and eye liner.

Poison was a biker by default, even though he hadn't ridden a motorcycle since kindergarten. A few months after he was born, his dad had attached a side car to the Harley.

Poison had one very clear memory of his biker days. He remembered looking up from that sidecar and watching his mother lay her head against his father's shoulder. Her long red hair had been tied back into a ponytail, but one strand had escaped and was flying about wildly. He remembered her oversized sunglasses. He remembered how she would reach down into the side car and wiggle her finger on his nose.

Most of Poison's friends said that remembering that far back was impossible—that he had dreamed it, or had seen it in a movie, and has somehow decided it was a memory. His mother, Brenda, remembered it very well, though—so she knew it was a true memory. This, as far as she was concerned, was just another sign of her son's innate brilliance.

The band called Poison had had a few hits along the way. Their song "Something to Believe In" was the lullaby she had sung to him as a baby. Poison's middle name was "Henry," after a grandfather he had never met.

Poison decided that, when (or if) he went to college, he would start using the name "Henry." Someday later on, when he had a corner office or was a famous artist, he would use the name "P. Henry Davenport."

Clients, or perhaps interviewers, would ask, "What's the 'P' stand for?"

Poison would smile slyly and say, "You wouldn't believe me if I told you."

The person asking would be intrigued and say, "Try me."

And Poison would tell them, and they would say, "No way."

Then Poison would take out his driver's license and show them. This was a scene he had rehearsed in his mind for years—he couldn't wait for it to finally happen.

Poison took his first steps at a bike rally in Tucson. His first solid food had barbecue sauce on it. One of his first words—right after "Mama" and "Dada"—was "Harley."

Poison's mother had been a teacher at one time. Then she had fallen in love with a man named "Snake," and had given it all up to ride around the country on the back of his motorcycle. (This was part of the reason Poison had never met his Grandfather Henry.) She had educated Poison herself until he was five years old. He had been reading Dr. Seuss when he was four.

The summer before Poison turned five, Brenda had decided it was time for the family to stop riding around, to buy a home, and to get young Poison into a regular school.

Poison's father's name was Snake. The name came from a tattoo that started at his right shoulder, disappeared down the back of his jeans, and came out on his left ankle. Snake had a passion for books. A small part of him, deep down inside, looked forward to the day when they would stop riding around: the day he could have books. Then he could have shelves of books if he wanted. He could have books in every room of the house that he would have someday. He could have book shelves in the bathroom. He could have piles of books on the counter, so that every time someone poured a cup of coffee in his house they would have to pick up a book and read for a few minutes. There was very little room for storage in a motorcycle sidecar, so other than a change of clothes, the only personal possessions Snake carried with him were a Bible and whatever other book he was reading at the time. He would stop at a used bookstore in some town along the highway, trade in what he had for something else, and then repeat the process whenever he was done. When Brenda had first met him, he had been lying with his head in the shade of his bike, reading Shakespeare.

When Brenda took a permanent seat behind Snake, the storage space grew smaller. When Poison was born and the sidecar became a crib, Snake bought a small trailer to hitch onto the back. When Brenda said it was time to stop riding around, they picked the town of Summer Park in Pennsylvania, got a loan from the bank, and opened a bookstore near the center of town. The building had a two-bedroom apartment upstairs—they lived there for their first ten years in Summer Park, eventually buying a house in the suburbs. Snake's real name was Edgar.

The store, which they named "Book 'Em, Danno," was a cozy place with several small rooms on the first floor. Customers could wander from room to room. The shelves, which Snake had built himself, reached from floor to ceiling. Every aisle had a stepladder. In the center, Brenda placed four full-sized sofas and three coffee tables, so that folks could sit and read. On those sofas, Poison did all of his homework. Every day, his mother would bring him a glass of ice-cold chocolate milk. Some of Poison's fondest memories were of the wide variety of people who sat down and helped him with his homework.

"Book 'Em, Danno" attracted the most eclectic clientele of any store in town. Teenagers came in looking for books they needed for school. Brenda started a book club for housewives who read romance novels. (Mrs. Pyle was in her eighties when she joined, and loved to read aloud the "good parts" as she called them. When she read about "heaving bosoms" or "flaming passions," she always seemed to be speaking from experience.) Poison liked the minister, who came by quite a lot. His name was Reverend Tumbler, and he would always smile kindly at Poison and ask, "How ya doin' there, young man?"

A lot of Snake's old friends stopped by. Some were still riding around—others now had more "respectable" jobs. Poison's favorite customer of all was a giant burly man whom his father called "Tuba."

Tuba once caught Poison adding with his fingers, and showed the boy how to multiply with them. Poison was multiplying and dividing before he got out of the first grade.

Poison's one holdover from his days as a biker baby was the inability to sleep when it was quiet. Silence at night drove him crazy, so he had purchased from the church rummage sale a metal fan for his bedroom. It whirred, rattled, and squeaked as it oscillated back and forth. He didn't use it to cool the room—it didn't actually spin fast enough to do that—but the sound put him to sleep as if he were still riding in the sidecar of Snake's Harley-Davidson.

And then there was that whole thing with the angels...

Poison had never told anyone about the angels. Something inside him (even at a young age) had warned him, "No one will believe you. Just keep your mouth shut for now." The very first angel he remembered seeing had been in the middle of the night, on the Christmas Eve that Tuba had died. He'd heard a noise in his room, and had woken up to see Tuba sitting on the edge of his bed, giggling like a two-year-old.

The mountain of a man, who had shown him how to multiply, was laughing so hard that he could barely keep his balance. A five-year-old Poison just stared at him. Tuba was in his trucker's clothes, but they looked brand-new. His wide-brimmed black hat—bought decades ago at a general store that catered to the Amish—looked so new it shone.

Standing next to Tuba was a man dressed all in white: twice as tall as Tuba, and his shoulders twice as broad as Tuba's own. Poison had seen pictures of angels in his children's story Bible, and there were several angel ornaments on his Christmas tree—but those angels looked serious. This guy looked so happy that he might explode. Tuba wiped his laughing eyes and said, "It's really beautiful."

Ever since that moment, Poison had been kicking himself for not having had the sense to ask, "What is?" He had just kept sitting on his bed in his Batman jammies, unable to speak.

Tuba had opened his broad arms, and Poison

had crawled out from under the covers and thrown himself into them. He had known, somehow, that Tuba was going away.

Poison had been sad, but only for a moment. When Tuba's huge hands had pressed against his back, Poison had felt a warmth surge through him, and he had known that everything was going to be okay.

That Christmas morning, the phone in the bookstore had rung and rung until Snake had finally gone downstairs to answer it. When he had come back up, he'd been crying. Poison's mother and father had held each other and cried for a while before telling their son. They had thought he would be sad—but then he had told them about Tuba coming to his room. Snake and Brenda had believed him—not in the way that adults sometimes say they believe when a child says something cute: they had truly believed him. Over the next several years, Snake had sometimes asked Poison questions: about what Tuba was wearing, or about what he had said.

Poison was seventeen now. Since Tuba's death, Poison had seen that same angel more than a hundred times. He had seen others too, but they had rarely acknowledged him. The angel who had brought Tuba to visit him would wave, though, and would sometimes give Poison the strangest dreams.

One day—it had been the first of November—that angel had spoken to him for the first time.

The angel had been hovering around Poison's room. Poison had been sitting on his bed, with his copy of Letters from the Earth open on his chest. It had been a school reading assignment. Poison had been enjoying the book, but he hadn't said so. Ms. Szuch had assigned that book because it was by Mark Twain. Poison had decided to go ahead and read it, because Ms. Szuch had said that it had been banned in some places and that Twain had gotten into a huge amount of trouble for writing it. Some schools, Ms. Szuch had said, still banned it

The other reason that Poison liked it was that it was about an angel. Most of the kids in his senior class, though, hated the reading assignments Ms. Szuch gave them. They also detested that she read to them aloud. What were they, first-graders? Poison, though, liked to be read to. He liked hearing the way she read, and sometimes it was her voice he heard in his head when he read to himself. He liked Ms. Szuch and always did his best for her.

The angel had appeared gradually, as if coming into focus: "phasing in," like actors standing in the transporter on Star Trek. Unlike the actors, though, the angel had not been standing still. He had been spinning around in a small circle, several feet above the floor. Even after he fully materialized, he seemed simultaneously real and unreal: transparent, yet somehow completely there.

The angel had studied the many paintings and sketches on Poison's wall. Many of them portrayed Poison's girlfriend Doreen. Some were of Poison's house—others depicted various things and people that Poison had drawn while sitting on the sofas in the bookstore. Several were pictures of angels.

The angel had scrutinized them all, as if trying to guess which of his friends each portrayed. Finally, the angel had stopped in front of one painting that had been exceptionally well done. It was of himself.

The angel had lowered into a standing position—well, not standing, but hovering close enough to the floor to give that impression. Then he had said, "Poison."

Poison had looked up at the angel, surprised for just a moment. He had sometimes wondered what an angel's voice might sound like. This one sounded human, but Poison seemed to hear the angel's voice from the whole room and not just from the angel's mouth.

The angel had called him by name. Poison had said, "This is going to hurt, isn't it?"

The smile had never left the angel's face, but his eyes had looked puzzled. "What do you mean, 'This is going to hurt?'"

Poison said, "All these years you've been hanging around—you and all your friends—not one of you has ever said a word to me. Now, you call me by name. So—if history has any accuracy at all, and if I remember my Bible stories—this is going to hurt."

The angel cocked his head slightly, as children do when they study something, or as anyone does when trying to figure out an abstract painting in a museum. He began to smile again and said, "Yes. This is probably going to hurt—but only for a short time, and only a little."

"Am I going to die?" Poison asked.

"Are you planning on throwing yourself off a cliff or something?"

"No," Poison said honestly.

"Then you'll be just fine," the angel replied. He floated up again to the painting of himself. "This is actually very good."

"You can keep it if you want," Poison said.

"No place to hang it."

The angel lowered again. If he was surprised at the casual way Poison had responded, he didn't show it. "I've never understood," he said, "why humans think they have to suffer to get close to God. Suffering comes, sometimes, when you ignore the Creator. God calls one of you to do something, and you go running off in the opposite direction. Then you get in trouble. You get hurt. You come running back, and do what you were told in the first place, and then go on and on about how much the trial brought you closer to God—when you should have just made the right decision before making the wrong one."

"We're a flawed creation," Poison said.

"Nothing the creator makes is flawed."

"But we make mistakes," Poison offered. "Big ones."

"That's your own fault. It's not a design flaw."

"So all our trials and tribulations over the centuries..."

"Are of your own creation." As the angel finished, he seemed to grow more solid somehow, as if filling in the space he occupied. "The human race has always made mistakes, when all the time you could have just done it the right way from the beginning."

"That would have made the Bible a lot shorter," Poison said.

The angel considered this, and nodded. "I am here with an assignment from the Almighty God."

"It sounds important."

"You think so?" The angel sounded sarcastic.

Poison smiled. Knowing that angels were capable of sarcasm somehow made him feel better about dying. He dog-eared the page in the book he was reading and put it aside. "So, what is it I'm supposed to do?"

"Christmas is coming."

"It's a ways away."

"That's time enough."

"For what?"

"Christmas has lost its meaning to a lot of people. Even those who consider themselves religious don't understand. They get caught up in being 'religious,' and forget what it's about."

"You mean it's not about toys and sales and Santa Claus?" (Poison had been thinking a little humor might be good right about then.)

"Nicholas is a good man. Don't disrespect him."

"Didn't mean to," Poison retorted. "I just meant...."

"I know," said the angel. "Keep your sense of humor; you're going to need it."

Poison suddenly had a mental picture of a cheap video box with the title "Poison Saves Christmas: A Family Favorite." He pushed the picture out of his head.

"Why me?" Poison asked. "Am I such a good person?"

"Better than some." The angel was now on the other side of the room—his face a few inches from a print of Vincent van Gogh's "Starry Night" that Poison had pinned to the ceiling. "Not as good as others."

"So, why me?"

"So, why not you?"

Poison sensed that this would be one of those conversations that went around in circles and never got him any answers. It was like the times he asked Doreen why she was mad at him, and she replied, "If you don't know, I'm not going to tell you."

"What does God want me to do?" He thought that this question was specific enough for the angel to give him a specific answer. Also, he was pretty sure that he didn't like the way the angel was looking around his room. It was as if the angel had just been let into the reptile house at the Pittsburgh Zoo.

The angel had turned to him and said, "The Creator wants you to use your gifts."

Poison had thought, "Nope. Nothing specific there." Out loud, he had replied only, "I don't suppose you'd like to be more specific."

"I don't suppose so, no."

"Am I supposed to start right away?"

"That would be preferable, yes."

Poison thought for a moment. He asked, "Is there a specific job I'm supposed to do—and I'm supposed to figure out what it is—or is it all up to me?" He thought that this would get the angel to choose one or the other.

"Use your gifts," the angel said again.

"Do I have to do this alone?"

"You're never alone," the angel shot back, smiling.

"I mean, can I get help with this assignment, seeing that I don't even know what it is?" Poison asked.

"Was that humor?"

"God doesn't like sarcasm?"

The angel continued, as if Poison had not spoken. "You can get help if you want to, but the more people you bring into this, the more chance you have of getting them hurt as well."

"Can I call you if I get in trouble?"

"Of course."

"What do I call you?"

The angel stopped floating and turned toward him. He bowed, just slightly, and said "My name is Bez-A-Lel."

"Will you come if I call?" Poison asked.

Bez-A-Lel the angel smiled a bright smile—and in that instant he was no longer there. There was no "poof"; there was no "Ta-daah!" or bright flash of light or cloud of smoke. One moment, he was there—and the next moment, he wasn't. Poison lay back down in bed and stared at the ceiling. He doubted very much that he could sleep—but in a moment he was sleeping more deeply than he had in years.

❄ ❄ ❄

Next morning, Poison wandered the bookshop. He usually went into the shop with his father before school—doing his morning job of re-shelving books that people had pulled out and left lying around. It was a family business. He had been "helping" since he was very small. His first job had been to sweep the sidewalk in front of the store. His mother had told him it was a very important job, so he did it as if it were the most important job. As he got older, he was also put in charge of cleaning the front windows of the shop.

When he was fourteen, he had asked his dad if he could paint pictures in the front window. His father had bought him a deck of cards with famous authors on the faces, and had told him that he could do one face per month, and that they would offer a discount to anyone who could guess the author portrayed. Poison had done so well on the portraits that his father had given him the job permanently.

Poison had practically grown up on the blue sofa. That was where he had learned to watch people. When he had been little, Rev. Tumbler from the community church had called him an "intuitive" child. Somehow, Poison could look at people and know if they were feeling angry, or sad, or were carrying something on their minds.

Poison worked for an hour before school every day and usually went straight to the shop after school. Lately, however, he had been going to a new coffee shop that had opened on the next block. That was almost the only time he got to spend with Doreen, other than lunchtime at school. After a coffee with Doreen, he would wander over to the book shop. There he would do his homework, and then help with inventory or whatever his father needed.

All morning, he had been watching people: trying to figure out who they were, and whether they were appreciating Christmas, and how he could use his gift to help them—if only he could find out what his gift was in the first place.

He had lost his concentration a few times, and had accidentally made a pot of coffee that had had twice the recommended number of scoops of ground coffee. Later, after the store opened, Mrs. Mallory (one of the romance group) took one sip and gasped as if someone had pinched her. Later, Snake told Poison to get his head out of the clouds and pay attention to what he was doing. It was something he heard from his father a lot lately: "Get your head out of the clouds."

(Snake tried repeatedly to get his son to focus on the life in front of him. Snake himself had been a dreamer. His own parents had been called into the school office several times for that: "Edgar lacks focus." He wanted his son to succeed. He wanted his son to have a better life. Yet, every time he turned around, the boy was daydreaming.

(One time, when Poison had been very young and Snake had been telling him to get his head out of the clouds and keep both feet on the ground,

Poison had asked: "If I keep both feet on the ground, how do I get my pants on?" Now, his son was seventeen and would be graduating from high school. Snake wanted to send the boy to college, but that would happen only if Poison kept his grades up and got a scholarship.)

Eventually, Poison decided that, if he was supposed to do some assignment as a servant of God, then God would show him what he was supposed to do. If he looked for it, he would never see it: kind of like seeing the angels. He would wait, then. Something would present itself. In the meantime, he had to tell somebody—or he knew he would explode.

Chapter 2

That afternoon Poison sat with Doreen. He held her hand and sipped his coffee. It was a drink that had three names, only one of which ("double") he knew the meaning of. It was overly sweet—he could barely taste the coffee. The top was covered in six swirls of whipped cream. Basically, it was a hot candy bar in a cup that he had paid three dollars for. He preferred the coffee in his parents' shop: a little cream in a white ceramic mug—75 cents, and the second one free: payments made to the glass jar with the hole in the lid sitting beside the coffee pot. He didn't understand how some places could get away with charging three dollars for coffee. It wasn't even coffee, really: the more expensive drinks had five or six words in their names. His three-dollar coffee was one of the cheaper things on the menu.

He had come into Hylander Coffee for the first time last year. It was one of those I'm-really-an-adult-now things he did with a group of other six-teen-year-olds. At first, Poison had thought the waitress had made a mistake. Then he had seen the looks on the faces of his friends and knew that they were sitting there, just as he was, trying to look like the bitter black liquid in the cup didn't bother them. He vowed never to drink at a Hylander Coffee again. Now here he was. He sat across the table from Doreen, his girlfriend of 18 months and four days. (She kept track.) He had just told her about the angels, about Tuba, and about the tall angel named Bez-A-Lel who had given him an assignment without actually giving him the assignment.

Doreen liked having coffee at Hylander's. She liked the atmosphere. She liked sitting outside when the weather was nice and sipping coffee. She always told him that someday she wanted to sit out on the street in Paris, sipping French coffee and watching the people walk by.

Poison knew he would marry her in an instant if he thought she would say "Yes." The fact was that he was afraid she might say "Yes," so he didn't ask her. She was smart. She was taking all the gifted programs at the school. He struggled and held on to his B average by the skin of his teeth, and most of that B was because of his straight A's in English and Art. He had no idea what he wanted to do when he got out of school. When Doreen talked about Paris, he never pictured himself next to her. He always pictured her there with some French guy. Doreen, on the other hand, never pictured herself in

Paris with anyone but Poison—and, although she tried to explain it to him, he couldn't get the handsome French guy hitting on his girlfriend out of his brain.

Doreen had eyes that, at first, he thought were contact lenses. Later, he learned that there really was a natural green that green. (This was one of the first compliments he had paid her, and it had been right on the money.) She also had a voice that had just a hint of an accent. Her mother had been born on "the Island," as she liked to say, and had moved here when she married Doreen's father. Doreen could slip into full "Island" mode as if flipping a switch. Poison found this adorable. (He had told her this once, and she had kissed him right out there in public). Doreen was the perfect blend of both her parents. Her hair was long and braided like her mother's; she had her father's practicality, and skin the color of the caramel coffee drinks that she liked so much. Doreen was talking about Harvard and Yale. Poison was talking about the art program in the community college, so that he could continue working at his parents' store.

Doreen's father called him "that boy" when he wasn't around. He had a tendency to sniff when he said Poison's name, as if he smelled the dust from the bookshelves or something else he found unpleasant. Poison had decided that he liked being called "that boy" who was from "that family," rather than "Poison (sniff)."

Poison and Doreen had met at a church youth event. She had been living on the other side of the state at the time. It was one of those big youth gatherings where youth groups show up from all over the state and drive their youth minister crazy by disappearing into the throng of bodies dancing to popular Christian music.

They had gotten along incredibly well the entire weekend and had spent most of it sitting and talking: just talking. When Doreen's father had received a job offer in Summer Park, they had moved—much to the chagrin of their teenage daughter. She had walked into her first day at a new high school without knowing a soul. When she had seen Poison in her homeroom, she had begun to smile. (Actually it was her first smile since she had heard they were moving.)

Poison and Doreen had been inseparable ever since. She was the one who had pointed out to him how often angels showed up in his art. She was the one who had told him that there was nothing wrong with wanting to be an artist. She was the one who had convinced him to enter one of his pieces in the Tri-County Art Show. (He took second place.) She had been good for him. He knew that. What he didn't know was exactly how good he had been for her as well. Until this moment, he had never told anyone about the angels.

She sipped her mocha-frappa-dappa-something and looked at him. "Okay," she said, "I'm saying this out loud so I know that I've got it, not because I don't believe you, okay?"

Poison nodded.

"You've been able to see angels since you were five years old, and the first time was when an angel brought a truck driver named Tuba to your bedroom."

Poison nodded again.

"You've never told anyone, because you were afraid they might send you to a doctor and he would medicate you to the point where you couldn't see them anymore."

Poison nodded. That particular part wasn't something he had said, but she was right.

"So finally, after about twelve years, an angel talks to you and tells you that you have to do some assignment that has something to do with Christmas but you don't know what it is—and he also said that if you brought other people into this they might get hurt."

"Yes," Poison said quietly.

"And you've decided to ask me to help you with this assignment that you don't know anything about."

Poison looked at her. Lately she had been wearing her hair down in black braids, instead of up in a ponytail. On the end of her nose was a single freckle, which he liked to stare at sometimes. He looked at her freckle, and then at her green eyes, and he said, "Yes, I'm asking you to help—even though I don't know what I'm supposed to do."

"Why?" she asked. It wasn't an accusation—she was just wondering.

"Because I really don't think I can do this alone, whatever it is."

She leaned across the table and kissed him on the cheek. "That's for sharing that with me," she said. She kissed him on the other cheek and said, "That's for trusting me."

Poison was always amazed at how long he felt the kiss on the skin of his cheeks when she kissed him. He would be feeling those spots for a few hours and he didn't mind. He was also aware that she had not yet said whether she believed him, or whether she would help him. "We might get hurt," he said.

"But you really think this is a God thing, right?"

Poison nodded.

"Okay, I'm in." She said it as if he had just invited her to go to the mall.

"You believe me?" he asked.

"Can I tell you something?"

"Sure."

"I was angry at God for a long time because of my dad. I didn't want to move. Then, when we moved, my grandfather died—and we weren't there when it happened. I told God I needed him to show me that he was real, and—if he was real—that he was doing something and not just sitting out in the universe watching and not caring. When my mom said we were moving, I thought for sure that just proved that God wasn't there at all. Then I walked into class and I saw you."

"So you're saying—" Poison smiled, sitting up a little straighter, "that I'm the answer to your prayer."

"Oh, please." Both Doreen and Poison looked

up at the waitress who had heard Poison's answer. She was a short woman, maybe 40—obviously the oldest employee at the café by about 20 years. Her nametag said "Molly." She had a rag in her hand and was wiping down the table where Poison and Doreen sat. Both teenagers obligingly lifted their cups and allowed her to clean under them. "Honey," the woman said to Doreen, "You just let them talk when they get like that. Just smile and nod your head. They all think, at that age, that they're God's gift to women."

"I'll remember," Doreen said.

Molly whispered, "Sometimes they grow out of it. Sometimes they don't."

A horn blasted, startling the three of them. They looked out the coffee shop's big picture window. A huge beige SUV was stopped in the middle of the road, about six inches from a very shocked-looking older man. The woman driving the SUV rolled down her window and screamed something before returning to her cellphone conversation. The man pulled his coat closer around him and kept walking. He got close to the curb and promptly stepped into a puddle that sloshed up over his ankle and filled his shoe. The man said nothing but looked heavenward as if he had just been the victim of some Godly prank.

"It's starting early this year," the waitress said.

"What's starting early?" Poison asked.

"Reverend Tumbler." She nodded toward the man in the long gray coat who was heading into the café. "The poor man just hates this time of year.

You would think the holidays were the favorite time of year for church folks, but Reverend Tumbler just seems to get more and more miserable every year."

The minister came through the door. He inhaled the smell of the coffee and baked goods, and seemed to feel a little happier. He shook one foot, wiped it on the entry mat, and walked over to the counter.

Behind the counter was a girl who seemed about 18. She asked, "Do you want the usual, Reverend?"

"Yes, that would be fine," the minister said in a quiet voice.

"Have a seat and I'll have someone bring it out."

"Thank you." The minister flapped his coat once or twice, as if either shaking off the cold or imitating a bat. He slipped out of his coat, and draped it across the back of a high stool at a tall table not too far from Poison's and Doreen's booth.

The woman who had cleaned Poison's and Doreen's table walked over to him and put down a cup of coffee. "Your bagel will be ready in just a minute."

"Thank you," the minister said.

Molly began to wipe down the table in front of him, even though it already looked clean. "Must be cold out there, eh, Pastor?"

"That it is, Molly. That it is." He let her finish her work. She seemed as if she wanted the conversation to continue, but when the minister didn't say anything else she walked away.

Reverend Tumbler turned to see Poison and Doreen holding hands in the booth. He smiled and nodded. Poison did the same back to him.

"I know you, don't I?" The minister said to Poison.

"Yes, Sir," Poison said. "You used to help me with my homework. My parents own that book-store on Main Street. We've been to church a few times—I was in the youth group for a little while."

"That's where I know you from," the minister said. He lightly slapped the counter. "You have an unusual name, as I recall."

"It's Poison, sir." Poison held out his other hand. The minister took it, and they shook.

The door opened again. A small man, not that much bigger than Poison, came into the café. Officer Royce looked around a little and then smiled. His smile was not a friendly one. It was one of those pasted-on smiles that make you think a person really wants to sell you the extra insurance package on that new stereo you just bought. He walked over and seated himself at the minister's table. The minister looked up, and Poison could tell from the look on his face that this was not a planned get-together.

"Are you okay there, Reverend?" Officer Royce said.

"I'm fine, Danny. Thank you."

"Are you sure?" the officer asked again. "I saw you walk out there in front of that truck. You ought to know better. 'Specially when you've got a woman driving with one of them cellphones attached to her ear. They don't pay attention."

"It was my fault, Danny," Tumbler said.

Officer Danny Royce chuckled, but he didn't get up, or even move. Officer Royce didn't like SUVs. He didn't like women drivers, and he didn't like cellphones. He didn't like dealing with small children. He didn't like slow-moving old people. He didn't like personalized license plates or people with tattoos. Officer Royce didn't like a lot of things. He didn't like teenagers. He didn't like immigrants (which there were only two of in Summer Park. The first was a woman named Nora: she was from Nigeria, and had been in town for four years. The other, technically an immigrant, was Doreen's mother.) Most of the teens at the high school had started calling him Officer Rhoid, as in "hemorrhoid." (The officer had the unpleasant task of giving the anti-drug lecture once a year at the high school. It had become a school joke.) Officer Royce didn't like ministers who wore white collars, as did the Reverend Tumbler. The officer had seen the reports on TV, and he distrusted anybody who hid behind a collar that way.

The eighteen-year-old from the counter brought over a plate with a steaming bagel. She looked at the police officer, but she didn't offer him anything. He didn't look at her either. If he had, he might have remembered that he had once brought her into the station house when she'd made a left turn on a red light. He'd given her a breathalyzer test, which she'd passed—but he'd brought her in anyway.

Reverend Tumbler muttered, "Can I get you a cup of coffee, Danny?" His offer was sincere, but the tone of his voice screamed I-REALLY-want-to-be-alone-so-please-say-no-thank-you-and-go-away.

"No, thank you there, Reverend," Officer Royce replied, and stood up to leave. "I just saw you walk out and almost get smashed there, so I thought I'd make sure you were clear-headed and sober—you know?" With this, he laughed and lightly punched the minister in the shoulder. It wasn't a real laugh or even a chuckle. It was fake, like saying, "You're really going to want that extra insurance on the rental car. Suppose you get hit by a meteor, heh, heh, heh." He was being sarcastic, but something in his voice made Poison think he would have liked nothing better than to find the minister had been drinking.

Officer Royce had a reputation at Poison's and Doreen's high school. It was one thing if Sheriff Forbes caught you doing something stupid, but another thing entirely if Deputy "Hemor-Rhoid" caught you.

Unless you were doing something dangerous or destructive, Sheriff Forbes would give you a quiet talking-to, and then suggest you spend some time at home. "Rhoid" preferred to take teenagers to the station house. He liked to go into the Seven-Eleven that had the "No More Than Three Students" sign on the door, because if you were number four, he'd take you to the station. He never arrested anybody for such trivial things—but he thought he was giving wayward youth a good scare to keep them on the straight and narrow.

Deputy Royce looked over at Poison's black leather jacket (a gift from his dad) and then, disapprovingly, at the hands holding across the table. Poison could see the wheels turning in Deputy Royce's mind. Royce looked from one teenager to the other, tapped his nose lightly, and grumbled, "You kids keep your noses clean, you hear?"

Doreen nodded. Poison didn't move, but kept his eyes on "Rhoid." The deputy spoke a little louder, "You show respect around the good pastor." With this said he pulled his hat down a little closer to his eyebrows and left the café.

Once Royce had left, the room began to move again. Poison looked around, and only then did he notice how things had stilled when the deputy had been in the room. He saw that Reverend Tumbler was looking around too. Tumbler looked at Poison quizzically: as if to ask, "Did you notice that too?"

Molly, the waitress, came over with her rag. "That man is such a pain in the caboose. 'Scuse my French, Pastor."

"I'm not sure 'caboose' counts as French, or as profanity for that matter, but you're excused." He paused and added, "Furthermore, you're right."

Molly playfully hit his arm and moved toward the kitchen.

Doreen patted Poison's hand and said, "I have to go—Shakespeare test tomorrow."

"That's tomorrow?" Poison asked, surprised.

Doreen looked at him. "Oh, yeah, you'll do just fine," she snickered.

"Which play?" Rev. Tumbler asked.

"Macbeth," Doreen told him, slipping her scarf around her neck.

"Ah. 'Tomorrow and tomorrow and tomorrow / Creeps in this petty pace from day to day / To the last syllable of recorded time / And all our yesterdays have lighted fools / The way to dusty death.'"

Poison and Doreen stared at him. He smiled. "I took Shakespeare in college."

"Give us something," Poison said.

The pastor looked at him. "Excuse me?"

"Give us something from a college class about the play, that we can use on the test because nobody else will know it," Poison said.

"Oh," the minister said. He bowed his head. Thinking. "Ummm…let's see. Okay…here, try this: say 'Tomorrow' over and over again."

Poison and Doreen said it together. "Tomorrow tomorrow tomorrow tomorrow tomorrow." They continued on, Poison stopping first, and then Doreen.

"Sort of loses its meaning, doesn't it?" Tumbler asked.

Poison nodded.

"So has life, by that time, for Macbeth. He's ready to kill himself there and then—and yet the word he chooses to say over and over is 'tomorrow.'"

Poison and Doreen looked at each other. They smiled, and then looked back at Rev. Tumbler.

"Plus," Tumbler continued, "You have the word 'tomorrow,' you have the word 'yesterday'—and you have the word 'today': hidden in the 'day to day.'"

"Thanks," Poison said.

"Don't mention it," said the minister, "Although I would go ahead and study if I were you."

"On our way," said Poison. He zipped up his leather jacket, Doreen pulled her big fuzzy mittens over her hands, and the two of them went out the door together.

Tumbler watched them go. He said to himself, "Life is a tale / Told by an idiot, full of sound and fury, / Signifying nothing."

"Did you say something, Pastor?" Molly asked.

"Nothing, Molly. Nothing at all."

Chapter 3

It was Friday afternoon. Poison stood outside. The weather was deciding whether or not it wanted to snow. First it wanted to, and then it didn't. Mostly the weather just decided to be cold. Poison switched the cardboard cup of coffee from hand to hand, to keep his fingers warm. He sipped the hot liquid, which helped—but not very much. He held it in his hands, knowing that this mini-furnace was his only source of heat right now. Poison had hoped the angel would light up his assignment with bright heavenly light and send a choir to sing a chorus of "Ahhhhhhhhhhs," but there was nothing. As he walked through town, he was on his own.

He stopped in front of the Summer Park Community Church, and watched as a group of volunteers built the traditional Nativity display. Poison remembered seeing this display every year since he had been a little kid. The wooden frame mock-stable surrounded the same Mary and the same Joseph. The same wise men stood nearby each year, the first one always kneeling. There were sheep and shepherds, and there was always one very big, very ornate angel that he liked a lot—but that didn't remind him of Bez-A-Lel at all. The figures were life-sized. He had checked, once, what they were made of: some ancient form of fiberglass. They were faded and scuffed, but had survived year after year of being shoved into an attic and brought out again to stand in the cold for November and December.

"Hey," yelled a large man. Everyone working turned to look at him. He was half bent over into a large dirty cardboard box. He was displaying an ample dose of butt cleavage for all to see. He popped his head out of the box and said, "Where the hell is Jesus?"

A group of older women who were working at cleaning the figures turned and whispered to each other. A group of men who were lashing the stable together with authentic Bethlehemian-looking rope started to smirk. The man who had yelled was still unaware of what he had just said. "There ain't no Jesus here," he yelled again.

A few people came over and looked into the box that the man had just looked into: as if maybe he had just missed a life-sized baby. This particular Nativity's baby Jesus, Poisoned remembered, did not have the traditional swaddling cloths. Presumably, it had kicked most of them off—except for one strip which covered what should be covered on a Savior. This church's baby Jesus did, though, possess a large metal halo that always reminded Poison of the take-up reel on the movie projectors at the high school.

Those who had come to investigate looked in the box and then at each other, and then agreed among themselves that—yes—it did, in fact, seem as though Jesus was AWOL.

They searched the other boxes and began to talk among themselves.

"We're going to need a new Jesus," the man with butt cleavage yelled to the group. He said it as if he had just run out of patience with the lot of them, as if he was putting the final point on an argument that hadn't occurred.

"We're going to need one new wise man, too," said a woman who was armed with a roll of paper towels and a bottle of Windex. She was standing over a collection of various figures.

"What's wrong with the wise man?" demanded a man in a red hat.

The woman with the Windex bent over and said, "It looks as if a family of mice made a home in his head this past summer. Most of his face is gone."

"Ewww," said a girl whom Poison thought to be about twelve.

"Is he a kneeling wise man or a standing wise man?" asked the man in the red hat.

"Kneeling," the Windex lady shouted back.

"Then we'll put him facing the manger for now." He said this with finality, as if he had just solved a major problem facing the world today. The name of the man in the red hat was Vaughn—Harry

Vaughn, to his few friends and many sycophants. He was the chairman of the church's property committee, and had a vice-moderator seat on the administrative board. He cared very much about his church, and had some strong opinions about who did and who did not live up to their responsibilities to the church...and to God, for that matter—and if the Lord Almighty wasn't willing to keep track of those who didn't live up to their responsibilities, then Harry was more than happy to fill in.

One of the Windex ladies said, "Maybe the property committee will buy a new set."

"Maybe we can just get the real wise men to come and stand in," someone else said sarcastically.

"This is an antique," Harry said. "You can't replace it. We'll have to have it restored."

The girl who had said "Ewww" chimed in: "Maybe we can get one of those light-up ones?"

The women around her smiled a series of oh-isn't-that-cute-someday-she'll-learn smiles, and went back to scrubbing the animals.

Poison watched this interaction from a distance. He had forgotten about his cold hands, and about the coffee which was no longer warm. He looked around briefly to see if Bez-A-Lel was there. Somehow, he just knew that this was his assignment. The wise man without a face, the serious deterioration of the other figures, the missing baby Jesus...this was what he was supposed to do. Somehow, he knew.

Coming toward the church on the sidewalk was the Reverend Tumbler. Tumbler had his hands jammed down into his pockets, a Cleveland Browns stocking cap on his head, and his coat was buttoned up over his collar. As he got closer, Poison saw him reach up and open his coat just a little: just so that his collar showed. It seemed to Poison that Tumbler was not trying to show it off, but that showing his collar was expected of him. Tumbler looked as if he would much rather have kept his coat closed during the winter in Summer Park, Pennsylvania. Poison thought the man would have been much more comfortable in a scarf to match the hat.

"Reverend Tumbler!" a woman called out. She had seen him first and wanted to be the first one to tell him that the baby Jesus was missing. She called his name in a sort of sing-song voice that made the other Windex ladies roll their eyes again.

"Good morning, Violet," Tumbler said. He lifted his head, so that his ears were exposed above his collar, and he winced at the wind.

"Reverend Tumbler," Violet said. "We can't find Jesus."

"Oh, I'm sure you will if you just keep looking, Violet," Tumbler said, with just a small trace of sarcasm that was lost on the woman. Poison—a connoisseur of sarcasm—caught it and smiled. Tumbler saw him smiling over Violet's shoulder.

"Really," Violet said, "we've checked the boxes and we can't find Jesus and one of the Wise Men is missing his face."

Harry Vaughn drifted over in his red cap and said in his most professional voice, "Well, we're probably going to have to have it restored next summer. Don't think there's time now."

"Well, that would be up to the property committee," Tumbler noted. He shivered as he stood there, hoping it might give the pair a clue that he was cold and wanted to be inside.

"Violet thinks we need a new one," Harry said. "I told her this one is an antique—we need to take care of it. A plastic replacement would look really cheap. This one has been around as long as I have."

Rev. Tumbler gave serious thought to asking if that also made Harry an antique. Instead, he offered, "Well, you can take it to the property committee tomorrow night. I'm sure you will all come up with an answer."

Harry smiled. As far as he was concerned, it was now a done deal. If anyone on the property committee took issue with the "restoration project," Harry would just tell them that Reverend Tumbler had agreed.

Tumbler started to move forward. Violet stepped backward to stay in front of him. "While you're here, Reverend," she said. "I was wondering if you had a moment to talk about the Christmas pageant."

"Doris Klimer is in charge of the pageant, isn't she?" Tumbler asked. He looked over to where the man with the butt cleavage was again bending over the box, as if somehow the Jesus figure had magically reappeared.

"Yes, she is," Violet said, "but have you seen the script? It's full of jokes, and she wants two of the teenagers to play Mary and Joseph."

"I think Mary and Joseph were teenagers," Tumbler said. "That might be a good thing: we can get some of the youth involved in the pageant."

"But the little ones so look forward to the pageant. It would be a shame to tell them that they weren't allowed to be Mary or Joseph."

From the way she said it, Poison guessed that she had a little girl whom she desperately wanted to see in the traditional Mary costume.

"Well, Doris is a capable woman, and very creative. I'm sure she has something wonderful in store for all of us." Tumbler started forward again, and again Violet stepped backward and started again to speak.

Poison interrupted: "Reverend Tumbler?"

Violet turned around: she was just a foot or so away from Poison.

Poison held out his hand. "I'm Joe Davidson. My mom set up an appointment."

Poison looked directly into the old minister's eyes, hoping he would catch Poison's look.

"Yes, Joe," Tumbler said. "I've been looking forward to meeting you. Let's go inside where it's warm." Tumbler smiled at Violet and walked around her with his hand on Poison's shoulder. The two of them headed for the door and Violet quickly scooted over to the ring of Windex ladies to see if any of them knew who the young man was, and what his parents did, and who the Davidson family was, and what anyone thought his problem was, and whether any of them supposed it could be drugs, and (if it was) who else was using them.

As they got closer to the door, Tumbler called out: "Ray, you let us know if you find Jesus." The butt crack man hitched up his pants, waved, and continued to stare into the empty box.

They walked through the door. Reverend Tumbler stamped the snow off his feet on the dirty foot mat.

"Shakespeare test, right?"

"Yes, Sir."

"How did it go?" Rev. Tumbler began flapping the arms of his jacket again.

"I won't know till after the Christmas break. I used the stuff you gave me, though. So did my girl-friend."

Reverend Tumbler took off his glasses and began to clean them with the end of his scarf. When he next spoke, he didn't look at Poison. "We don't have an appointment, do we?"

"No, sir," Poison said, "You looked cold."

"You're very quick," Tumbler said. "Was the Joe Davidson reference on purpose? Because Joseph was of the house of David?"

"Yeah." Poison said.

"Did you make that up on the spot?"

"No," said Poison. "I think I read it some-where."

"You read a lot?"

"My parents own a bookstore."

"How come I don't see you in church?"

Poison was silent. He started to say something, and then held back.

Tumbler said, "This is where you say, 'I'd really like to, Reverend, but my parents don't get up and I'd feel awkward going by myself without my loving family.'"

"Yeah, that works," Poison said.

"You're always welcome," Tumbler said. He pulled his glasses off again, as if he was trying to see the smudge that was there when they were on his face but not when he took them off. "So, did you really want to talk or are you going to sneak out the back door?"

"I'll go out the back, if you don't mind," Poison said. "It was good to meet you."

Poison held out his hand. He could barely keep from smiling. He knew what his "mission from God" was. He knew what he was going to do. Scratch that...he knew what he was supposed to do. He was hoping Bez-A-Lel would show up again, so he could tell him about it.

Tumbler watched the young man go out the back door and down the street. He stomped his feet a few more times and headed for his office. He passed Mary Jane: the secretary/receptionist/office administrator/security guard and—if the occasion called for it—human attack dog. She was on the phone, but she waved and held up a stack of pink "while-you-were-out" message papers. He smiled and took them from her. She had been a real gem. She knew exactly what had to be done and when. She kept him in line like a Cub Scout den mother sometimes. She hated to be called "secretary," but she insisted on a card and lunch on "Secretaries' Day." She made great coffee, but he told her she never had to bring him a cup unless she was getting one for herself. He got one for her whenever he got one for himself. They seldom traded personal stories. He knew her family and what they did. She had always been polite to his wife, and cooed at his baby, and she kept Dum-Dums in her desk drawer for whenever kids were in the office, and she saved the butterscotch ones for him. Since the accident, she had been incredibly professional. She had kept the church running during the three months that he had basically dug himself a hole and hid there. She knew how to keep church business confidential: didn't mind occasionally saying, "He's not in his office" when they both knew that's where he was. She loved office gadgets: things that stapled, fastened, glued, and fixed. She loved learning new software on the computer system, and she loved the fact that only she understood it. She had stretched the budget so thin that, by this time of year, they were both bringing in coffee, pens, paper, and various other items from home.

There had been one episode, a few years earlier, when Violet had told him that Mary Jane was coming in late and leaving early, and that Mary Jane was quietly informing others in the congregation who was giving the most money and who had cut back on their offerings.

Tumbler knew about the leaving early and the coming in late. These coincided with her husband's unemployment and her daughters' starring role in *The Music Man* at the high school. Tumbler also knew that Mary Jane had an uncanny ability to type meeting notes without reading them: notes would go directly from a notebook to the computer, misspellings and all. He also knew that she had nothing to gain from telling anyone who gave and who didn't. Finally, Tumbler knew that the accusations came a few weeks after Violet's son's name was left out of the Sunday bulletin on Confirmation Sunday.

The board convened. Reverend Tumbler began the meeting with all of this information, and the matter was dismissed quickly—but Violet had not given Mary Jane the time of day since then.

He walked to his office and saw a dozen yellow sticky notes with things he had to do. A pain began inside his temple, and he flopped heavily down into his chair.

"Reverend Tumbler!" a voice came from outside. Tumbler looked out his office window and saw Violet waving a naked baby in the air. "I found Jesus!" she shouted.

"Hallelujah," he called through the glass, and began to return his phone calls.

Outside, Poison had to keep himself from breaking into a run. He was so pumped he couldn't stand still. He would restore the Nativity himself. He could do it. He was sure. He almost said this to the minister, but he also knew the can of worms that it would open up. He would do this on his own. The town would think it was some kind of miracle. Well, maybe not really, but it would become some sort of legend. Pieces would disappear and then return as good as new...better than new. It would call attention to the church. People would take notice. They would think about what was going on in the church and not in the mall. Yes, he liked this idea. He liked this idea a lot. He stood and looked up at the sky: "Is this it?" He half hoped for a flash of light or a giant hand to give him the okey-dokey sign, but there was nothing. He kept moving. He didn't need the okay. This was his assignment, and he knew it. He would do this on his own, and would tell no one. "Okay," he said aloud, "Almost no one."

❊ ❊ ❊

"I'm in," Doreen said. She said it before he was done explaining his plan.

It was later now. They were walking through downtown. The Christmas lights were up on the tree in the center of the park. It was a great night for a walk: cold, but no wind. The flakes of snow were coming down like large six-pointed ornaments. They rested in Doreen's braided hair, but didn't melt right away. She wore one of those heavy headbands that covered her ears, but that didn't sit on her head like a stocking cap. It matched her mittens. Her winter coat was new as well.

Sometimes Poison wondered if there was any chance he would ever be able to make this girl happy for the rest of her life. He'd marry her, but he was a guy who'd been wearing the same leather jacket for years. It had been too big for him when his father gave it to him. This was the first year it fit him just right.

She had taken off one mitten so she could feel the skin of his hand, and they kept both hands in his jacket pocket.

"I don't know if you should," Poison said. "I probably shouldn't have told you. The angel said it could hurt. I don't want you to get hurt."

"You brought me into this," Doreen said.

"Yeah, but look at the stories. You don't hear a lot about Noah's wife or the girlfriends of the prophets. Most of those guys went off on their assignments alone. They didn't drag someone else along."

"Mrs. Noah went along," Doreen pointed out.

"Yeah, but other than 'take your wife,' what part did she play? What was her name?"

"You're very knowledgeable for someone who didn't go to Sunday School."

"My parents own a bookstore," Poison said. "You don't think I read? Sure, there were a lot of women heroes in the Bible—but mostly, they didn't go along with the guys on assignments. Moses took his brother. Elijah took Elisha. Jesus took twelve guys."

"And Mary and Martha."

"But you don't hear about them after the big

Easter story. It's not like they went off with Peter or Paul."

"They probably did, but the women didn't get full credit in the Bible," Doreen said. "None of the great prophets could have pulled off their assignments alone. I'm in, I told you."

"I don't want you to get in trouble," Poison said.

"Maybe we won't. Maybe we'll be just fine."

Poison didn't say anything. He just looked at the ground.

She leaned in close and put her head on his shoulder. "What do we do first?"

"Well," he said, "first we have to get the statues. Put them in the garage, where I have all my art stuff. We can do the work there. I'll tell my folks to stay out because I'm working on a Christmas present."

"Okay—question."

"Shoot."

"If it takes you a few days to fix and repaint the figures, what do you think is going to happen when people see the figures are missing?"

"I'm going to put them back."

"Yes, but the police don't know that," Doreen reminded him. "You don't think the Rhoid is going to launch a full-out investigation? And Rev. Tumbler doesn't know you'll be putting them back. You may start off making things worse for him— and he's the one you think you're supposed to help."

Poison hadn't thought about it. "Things might get worse before they get better," he admitted, "but nobody said it was going to be easy. Once the figures start coming back, people will see it as a miracle."

"People will see it as theft," Doreen murmured.

Poison nodded. She was probably right. He was grateful for her warm hand. He looked at her while she studied the falling snow. Never once had she questioned whether or not he had actually seen an angel. Never once had she questioned this "assignment" he was on. Never once had she questioned whether or not he was a talented enough artist to pull this off. Even if he had questioned his ability to do this—she had not.

They crossed the street and headed toward the church: a tall white building, with six steps leading up to its green door. The building itself had been put up in the 1930s. In the 1960s, another building had been added behind the original, to serve as Sunday school classrooms. After that came a meeting hall and offices. Reverend Tumbler's office, though, remained in the sanctuary building. You could see right into his office from the street. There had been some talk when he put up window shades. He'd said it was because it was difficult to work with the morning sunlight coming in. A few folks wondered what it was he had to hide.

There in the front yard stood the Nativity. There was a pair of spotlights on above the doors, but only one of them worked. Right now, it illuminated the half of the yard where the Nativity wasn't. Poison and Doreen stood there looking.

In the center of the yard sat an eight-by-eight-foot shed. Actually, it was mostly the frame of a shed—had anyone actually tried to use it as a stable, the results would have been the same as sleeping outside. Some church members thought they should put a roof and sides on the frame, but another group said that the shed was merely representational of the stable, so if the "roof-and-sides" faction was willing to pay the cost of lighting the stable to let Mary and the baby be seen, then the "representational" faction would be all for putting a roof and sides on the stable. For the moment, the framework stood as it had stood since the 1930s. A four-foot-tall Mary figure knelt reverently at the manger. She was dressed in the classic blue robe and white headdress. A tarnished brass halo encircled her head. It matched the projector reel around her son's and her husband's.

Joseph stood next to the manger on the other side. As in all great portraits of Joseph the adoptive dad, he appeared to have nothing to do. In art, sometimes Mary has held the baby: at other times, she has knelt with her hands open as if gasping in awe at the child. But most of the great Nativity art has depicted Joseph merely standing by the manger, doing nothing at all but looking stoic: as if he had been hired to be the Lord's anointed bouncer standing there in case any shepherds or animals should get too close.

There were two shepherds off to the right of the shed. Each held a staff. Both appeared to be made from the same mold as Joseph, with a different paint job. If not for the paint job, they could have been twins to each other and triplets to Joseph. In 1981, someone had painted a mustache on Shepherd #2. The chairman of the Christian Education committee had repainted the face: ever since, Shepherd #2 had looked as though he was wearing lipstick.

The most detailed of the figures were the wise men. The one whose face was missing knelt at the manger. Poison pointed this out to Doreen: "If you were a baby, and looked up and saw that face, what would you do?"

Doreen smirked. "Maybe that's what Mary seems so surprised at."

Poison asked, "Do you know which wise man is which?"

"What do you mean?"

"I mean, isn't one of them named Balthazar or something like that?"

"That's legend," Doreen said. "The Bible doesn't give them names. The Bible doesn't even say that there were three of them. All it says is that there were three gifts. It could have been five wise men, and two of them didn't get mentioned."

"Probably because they didn't bring a gift," Poison offered.

Nailed securely to the top of the shed was an angel. "The angel will be the hardest to remove," Poison said, "and probably the hardest to return."

In the center of it all was the baby Jesus, who once was lost and now was found. The baby lay in a wooden manger of real hay. The hay had been ordered from a church catalog that offered religious and Nativity supplies directly from Bethlehem. The hay came from a field not far away from the actual place where the stable had been. Some thought it was wasteful; others thought it was a nice touch to have "real Jesus" hay in the manger, as opposed to the stuff that any of the farmers in the community could bring in off their field.

Baby Jesus was white and almost blond. He held his arms up, as if he either was blessing the animals in the stable or needed to be picked up and changed. Like every other figure in the set, Jesus was made of a thick, high-grade fiberglass.

"So what's first?" Doreen said.

"I think I'll take the shepherds," Poison said. "I can probably use one of them to make a mold, so I can make a new face for the wise man."

"I think they're twins," Doreen said. "What does it matter which one you use?"

"Well, look at the guy on the right. I think he's wearing makeup."

Doreen started to smile. "Must be the black sheep of the family." She covered her face with her hand and laughed into her mitten. Poison just slowly turned his head and looked at her. "I don't believe you just said that."

"It was pretty baaaaaaaaaad, wasn't it?" She was laughing now. She let go of his hand to steady herself on his shoulder, the laughter having made her dizzy. When she finally calmed down, Poison asked, "Are you finished?"

"Yes, Mr. Da Vinci."

"Da Vinci did the Last Supper. It's the wrong time of year."

"Who did the Nativity?" Doreen asked.

"God," Poison retorted. "You keep a lookout. I'll go get the van."

A few minutes later, Poison pulled his father's van up near the front yard of the church. Doreen had scouted the place out. They were the only ones on the street. Poison jumped out and stood beside her. From this spot they both could see the front of the police station on the corner of Elm and Park Avenue. There was a light on, but no movement inside or outside.

All this time, Poison and Doreen had stood on the sidewalk, never actually venturing into the yard in front of the church. Now, Poison moved forward as if he was entering a minefield. He placed a hand on the shoulder of the six-foot-tall shepherd and gently rocked the figure slightly back and forth. It wasn't attached to the ground by anything except its own weight. "They should find a way to bolt these things down," Poison said. "Somebody could come along and…oh, yeah."

It wasn't too incredibly heavy. Poison took the feet, Doreen took the head, and they carried the shepherd across the yard and carefully placed it lying down in the back seat. They went back for the second one. Within a few minutes, they were on the road and driving toward Poison's house.

"Holy crap, that was easy," Poison said.

"This is a small town," Doreen reminded him. "Everything shuts down at eight. People want to be home to watch America's fine television programs and go to bed."

"I hope the rest of it will be this easy."

"I wouldn't count on it," Doreen said.

Poison turned and looked at the two shepherds lying in the back of the "Book 'Em, Danno" van. He suddenly felt a sick feeling in the pit of his stomach.

"We're criminals," Doreen said.

"They won't catch us. We're on a mission from God," Poison reassured her, doing his best to sound like Dan Aykroyd.

"Quoting movies in which the characters went to prison is probably not what I need for reassurance."

"You don't have to be involved."

"I am involved."

"You're not involved if I get caught," Poison said. "It's better that way. Your parents already don't like me. If they think I got you involved in the theft of holy relics, they will definitely not let me take you to the prom."

"Since when did you want to go to the prom?"

"I don't. I thought you did."

"Have I ever struck you as a prom queen?"

Poison sat for a moment. This was one of those questions. He knew better than to give a straight answer. He also knew he was running out of seconds to answer in.

"Well," he said, "I guess I was just looking forward to seeing you in one of those fancy dresses."

He waited, counting the seconds.

"Oh," she said. "That's so sweet."

("Yes!" he thought.).

"You're also full of crap," she said.

("Ewwwwwwwww. He misses the putt," Poison thought.)

They drove silently for a while, each of them taking turns glancing into the back seat. "The kids are awfully quiet tonight," Poison said.

"It was a long day." Doreen said.

Poison looked in the rear view mirror. The shepherd who looked as if he were wearing lipstick seemed to be looking back at him. His plaster facial expression seemed to say, "You are so busted."

They slowed down as they pulled into Poison's driveway. Moving quietly, Poison and Doreen unloaded one shepherd, and then the other. They stood them in the corner of the garage, and Poison covered them with some old drop cloths that his family had used when they painted the house last summer. As they came out of the garage, Poison held Doreen's hand. The back door of the house opened, and Poison's mother looked out. "Doreen, your mother is on the phone. She says you were supposed to be home a while ago."

"I'm on my way," Doreen said. "Isn't the first big snowfall romantic?" She used her I'm-such-a-ditzy-girl voice hoping Poison's mother would repeat it back to her mother on the phone. Poison's mother shut the back door. Poison and Doreen could see her talking on the phone again.

"You don't have to do that," Poison said.

"Do what?"

"Pretend to be a dumb blonde to my mother."

"It gets me out of trouble sometimes," Doreen said. "And what did you think she thought we were doing in the garage?"

The door opened again, and Poison's mother held out the cordless phone to Doreen. Doreen walked up the back steps, smiled her "Oh, well" smile to Poison's mom, and tried to take the phone with her mittens on. She almost dropped it, and finally took her mittens off. "Mom?" She went back down the steps, and Poison came up.

"Mom," he said. "I need you and Dad to stay out of the garage if you can."

"Why?" his mother said. She didn't say it accusingly—she just wanted to know.

"A Christmas secret." He smiled at her like a kid who was hiding a piece of construction paper with a ton of glitter and glue.

His mother looked at him for a moment and then said, "You need to get her home. Her mother is mad. You need brownie points."

"All we were doing was walking around downtown," Doreen said. "It's a beautiful night...yes...we were just walking....Mo-ther!"

Poison looked back at his mom. She said, "You really need brownie points."

"All we did was walk around. Really," Poison said.

"Talk to your father," his mother said "His girlfriend's parents didn't like him much either. Your grandparents hated your father, and they lost out on an entire part of their daughter's life." She looked at him and said, "If she's the one, you find a way to make it work."

Poison smiled. He looked over at Doreen, who seemed to be pleading with the sky as she talked. She made a horrible face, and then pretended to scream. "Daddy, how am I supposed to be on my way there when you've kept me on the phone here for the last ten minutes?" She looked at Poison, her eyes pleading. He made a what-can-I-do gesture.

"Yes, I know...Yes....Yes....not for the whole day, no.....because Poison invited me to come to his house for supper on Saturday....Yes, I did tell you about that."

Poison looked at his mom. "Is it okay if I invite Doreen over for supper on Saturday?"

Brenda said, "Well, as long as you checked with me first. We're having the last of the turkey left-overs...quesadillas, I think." Doreen was spinning around in the yard, pinching her face as if she had a headache. "I'm going to give the phone back to Mrs. Davenport now, Dad...yes...I'm coming right home...I'll run for the car as soon as I give her the phone. Goodbye, Daddy." Doreen handed the phone to Poison's mother and calmly walked to the car where she pretended to beat her head against the hood.

"Ted?" Poison's mother said. "Yes, she's on her way. I'm watching her get in the car...okay...thank you...Ted, I will....You have a Happy Thanksgiving too."

Brenda switched off the phone and said, "So, you're going to come over to supper on Saturday? That will be nice."

"I'll be there," Doreen said. "One way or the other, I'll be there. I'll remind my father a few hundred times between now and tomorrow night, and he'll tell me how far my grandparents travel just to see me, and then he'll tell me how holidays are meant for family. My Aunt Helen comes over and my uncle and cousins. Then we all go over to Aunt Helen's on Christmas. We almost never see them the rest of the year. Then it's twice in two months. Mom and Aunt Helen stay in the kitchen to complain about Grandma. Grandma complains to me about Aunt Helen and Mom. My cousins sit and play video games on one TV while my uncle watches football on the other TV and drinks beer."

"Sounds festive," Brenda said.

"Sounds like family," Doreen said.

Brenda nearly beamed with pride when she watched her son open the car door for his girlfriend. She resisted the urge to make an oh-isn't-that-cute face and then run and get the camera.

"I'll be back in a bit," Poison said as he walked around the car. "Tell Dad about the garage. Okay?"

His mother waved and disappeared inside. Poison backed out of the driveway and headed toward Doreen's house. They drove quietly for a moment. Poison steered with one hand and held Doreen's hand with the other. Her hand felt good to him, more than good. It felt right. She asked, "Do you think your parents would believe you if you told them what you were doing?"

"I think they would ask a lot of questions, and

eventually I would find a way to talk myself out of doing this—and I don't want to do that. Doing this feels right."

"Have you thought about what to do if it all goes south on you?"

"No."

"Servants of God have no backup plans?" she asked.

"If it's God's plan, then you don't need a backup. It will happen."

"But it might hurt," she said, quoting what he said the angel had told him.

"Yes."

"And servants of God who bring their girlfriends along risk getting their girlfriends in trouble as well."

"Yes." Poison said.

"You'd better be sure about this, Angel Boy," Doreen said. It was the first thing she said that could have been taken as being even a little skeptical. He listened to her voice for any trace of doubt or fear, but there was none. She had complete faith in him. In a way, he had been hoping that maybe there might just be a slight trace of questioning in her tone. It might make it easier to tell her that he was starting to get scared himself.

Chapter Four

Doreen stood in front of the door to her house, knowing her father would be waiting for her. She also knew Poison would wait until she got inside. He had offered to walk her to the door, but she had told him that her father was already upset and that things would work out better if he stayed in the van.

Her father would be pacing the floor, wearing a rut in the rug, until he saw the lights of the Davenport family van pull into the driveway. He would then rush to his chair and pick up a book and clutch it so tightly that his knuckles would turn white. He would pretend he was calm.

Doreen's mother often said that her husband was going to have a stroke from being so "calm" all the time.

Ted Hudson was a practical man in almost all things. All questions could be answered logically. All unexplained events had an explanation.

Foolishness was not accepted. Artists were like a box of granola. What wasn't flakes or nuts was fruits. Ted Hudson believed in what he could see in front of his face. If one could not see it, taste it, touch it, hear it, or smell it, it did not exist.

He sat in his chair trying not to vibrate in his frustration. His daughter had been out with "that boy" again: the one who looked like a biker but memorized Shakespeare. The one whose family owned an entire bookstore that was ninety percent fiction. The rest was out-of-date financial books and biographies. Ted Hudson could see the merit in a biography. You could learn something from that. You could see how other people faced life, and how they succeeded or failed, and you could learn from that. But "that store" with "those people" who had raised "that boy" had six entire bookcases of romance novels. Ted had come to call these books, affectionately, "pure crap."

As a boy, Ted had come to trust numbers. His parents had spent a lot of time lying to each other and lying to him. They would smile and drag him from place to place and pretend to be the great all-American family. He would lie in bed at night and listen to them yell at each other in the next room. His mother's smile became so plastic and false he learned to quit listening to her whenever she smiled. Once he woke up to find her making his favorite breakfast, French toast. Somewhere between his third and fourth slice, she told him that his father had left and it was going to be just the two of them from now on. Ted finished his breakfast and got ready for school. On his way, he quickly left the sidewalk and threw up in the bushes.

Numbers didn't lie. 2 + 2 would equal 4, no matter what you did. Numbers had certainty. Numbers had consistency. Numbers did not lie. Ted came to love numbers, and excelled in all things mathematical. He left home the day after his high school graduation, and got his degree in Applied Mathematics. He went to work for Bruce Harper, Certified Public Accountant. Within five years, it was Harper and Hudson, Certified Public Accountants. Within ten years, it was Hudson Accounting. Ted spent his day with numbers: putting them in rows, rearranging them so they would be easier to use, sorting them into different files— and always, always, always making sure they added up to what they were supposed to add up to. One answer. No arguments. Numbers did not lie.

The only areas of his life in which he was not a practical man were with his wife and, just lately, his only daughter. His daughter grew more and more beautiful every day and he worried about her, protected her like a bear. When she was small, he would tell her "the way things are" and she would say, "Okay, Daddy."

That stopped about the time she was 12, when she had learned the best way to get under his skin was to say "Why?" It maddened him.

Getting married was the most impractical thing that Ted Hudson had ever done. At least, getting married the way he did was impractical. When Mr. Harper discovered that Ted had not taken a vacation in five years, he simply ordered Ted to stay away from the office for two weeks. Ted had every intention of working from home for that time, but his boss presented him with an airline ticket and a reservation to an "Island Get-Away Resort." Mr. Harper had also ordered him not to take his wristwatch or his alarm clock, and to leave any work at home. Ted protested, but his boss (and future business partner) would not accept anything but full obedience on this one—so Ted went.

He spent the first day by the pool, pretending to relax. He was as white as a carp, lying there by the pool. He slathered himself with sunscreen and lay there for two hours, turning every fifteen minutes to get an even tan. Two hours later, he got up and took a walk. He shopped for nearly a full half-hour. By the end of his first day, he was sitting in his hotel room watching CNN and checking the Yellow Pages to find a place where he might be able to send a fax and get his secretary to mail him the Lawrence reports without Mr. Harper knowing. Mr. Harper, knowing Ted Hudson, had forbidden his secretary to send any such correspondence in the event that his colleague called.

The second day of his vacation, Ted Hudson went for a long walk off the beaten path. About noon, he walked into a tiny open-air restaurant and fell in love. His waitress looked him over and smiled. She had long rows of hair the color of solid ebony. It hung down around her dark shoulders. Her sundress was an exotic print, which she wore partly open and tied with a fabric belt. He learned later that she had made both the dress and the belt herself.

He ordered shrimp. She brought it to his table.

He invited her to sit down and share it with him. She did.

She said her name was Iza.

He had never seen such eyes before. He had never seen a smile like hers. He asked her how long she had been a waitress.

He learned she was a waitress only during the summers, when she was not teaching. Her family owned the open-air restaurant, and she had been working there with her family for as long as she could remember.

For the next two weeks, they spent every waking minute together. She asked him about all the things he did in America, and he honestly couldn't tell her anything he did outside of work. "Poor t'ing," she said, as she touched his face one night.

"So much life to live and you don' wan' to be livin' it."

She was right. He had felt more alive this past few weeks than he had in the twenty-seven years he had been alive. He told her so, and she smiled for him.

He had learned that when she smiled he felt better, so he did everything he could to make her smile.

He invited her to come home with him. She said, "No." He told her that he would stay and open up an accounting office here. She said "'Less'n you workin for de 'otel, people 'round 'ere ain' got much to be countin'. And da people who do 'ave money on de island are people you don' wan' to be workin' for."

For just a moment he thought to himself that she didn't really have any feelings for him—that she thought of him as a "fling." Then, on the night before he left, she wept against his shoulder until he found himself weeping too.

He wrote his first letter to her on the plane ride home. He mailed it from a mailbox outside of the Pittsburgh airport. It was 11 pages long. He wrote a second letter the next day. On his lunch break, he went out and had his film developed and bought a frame for every picture of her that he had. There were thirty.

Everyone commented on the change in him. Everyone said he must have had a wonderful time. When they asked to see his vacation pictures he realized that there were only two that did not have Iza in them. He finally confessed that he had met a beautiful woman on the island and endured the jibes and jests of all those who knew him. Then they saw the pictures of the girl, and they started asking when he was going to go back.

Ted wrote to her every day for two months. She wrote back on stationery that smelled like coconut tanning lotion.

He spent three days writing her a poem. He put it into a padded envelope, with a plane ticket and a diamond ring. The ring had cost him only $25—he promised that he would buy her a more expensive one if she came to America and agreed to be his wife. Doing it that way was more practical than purchasing an expensive ring up front.

It was a happy man who met her as she got off the plane. It was a happy man who immediately got down on one knee and proposed with an even larger diamond.

She laughed and touched his face and said "Yes."

Now, Ted Hudson was an upper-middle-class, slightly balding, white man in his forties. Iza had not just come in and become a part of his life—she had given him life.

She had also given him a daughter who looked like the beautiful teacher/waitress he had met on an island far away. Her hair and her face were like her mother's but her skin was lighter. It made her eyes seem darker. Summer Park, Pennsylvania, had embraced this mixed-race family. Oh, a few eyes in the church narrowed when they attended, but Ted did not care—and Iza had no qualms about shooting a narrow-eyed look back at the line of old women who stared at her, and at pretty much everything else in the world, with distrust. Iza got her teaching certification and began to teach art at the elementary school. They were the art teacher and the accountant, two vastly different people, whom God in his infinite wisdom (and sense of humor) had chosen to put together for life.

About five years ago (while his daughter was just growing out of her "Yes, Daddy" years), Iza called Ted into the dining room and sat down with him at the table. She had a large sheet of paper in her hand. She placed it between them. She had drawn a pencil sketch of the two of them waltzing. She had also made a list of all his favorite foods.

She said, "Do you know w'at dis 'ere picture is?"

He said that it was of the two of them dancing.

She said, "You close. Dis picture is of you an' me dancin' at our gran'baby's weddin'."

He smiled. "I look pretty good for an old guy."

She pointed to the list of his favorite foods. "Dis lis'," she said, "All t'ings dat make you fat an' close up your arteries and make your cholesterol go t'ru da roof. Less'n you do somt'ing about dat, den you ain' gonna be dancin' wit' me at de weddin' of our gran'baby."

He looked again at the list. It was all of his favorite foods.

"So I'm gonna make you a deal, pale boy," she said. "I want you to look at dis lis', and I want you to pick one t'ing. One t'ing that you like mos' of all. Den, every time you have dat one t'ing, I ain' gonna say a word. Everyt'ing else on da lis' is gone. You don' git it no more. Maybe once in a while, but mostly it's gone from your diet."

He looked at the list again.

She said, "I mean dis. I know dis is hard, so I'm gonna give you a few days. Dere ain' no way I'm gonna dance by myself at my gran'baby's weddin'. You ain' gonna leave me alone to do dat."

She got up from the table and kissed him full on the lips. He kissed her back, and he remembered how hard it had been to leave her once. He wasn't going to do that again—at least, not without a fight.

He studied the list for two days, and finally chose pie. She said, "Okay. We have a deal."

She was true to her word. They would go out to eat, and he would order pie for dessert, and she didn't raise an eyebrow. The house was soon devoid of all chips, cookies, puddings, and ice cream. Chicken was grilled, not fried—vegetables were lightly covered with a low-fat butter-like spread. He'd lost nearly forty pounds the first year. One night as he was weighing himself, she saw that he was holding up his shorts with his hand so they didn't fall down around his ankles. "You have de nice ass for a white man," she said. He laughed. He was looking forward to dancing with her at their grandbaby's wedding.

But for them to dance at that wedding, they first had to have a grandchild—and to have a grand-child, they would have to have a son-in-law—and to have a son-in-law, they would have to have a wedding. And to have a wedding, he would actual-ly have to let his daughter have a boyfriend. He decided it was okay for her to date whomever she wanted to—as long as it wasn't "that boy."

He watched her through the little window in the front door. "Boy won't even walk her to her front door," he thought. "Little twerp." He saw her com-ing, dived for his chair, and picked up his book: Wright is Right. He had finished it a few days ago, but it was too late to grab anything else. He made sure it wasn't upside down, and waited for her to come in.

She came in and hung her winter coat on the

hook near the door. She toed out of her boots and stepped over the spot where she had tracked snow on the welcome mat. She padded into the living room. "You don't have to wait up for me," she said.

"I wasn't waiting up," he said "I was reading."

"You've finished that book."

"I'm re-reading the parts that I like."

"That guy is a racist! How can you stand him?"

Ted Hudson looked at the cover of his book. From the cover, the young man in the power suit looked back. "He's not a racist, Honey. He tells it like it is."

"He makes stuff up."

They'd had this argument before. He didn't want to have it now. If he got angry now, he knew he'd say something about "that boy," and then she wouldn't hug him goodnight. He loved her hugs. Ever since he'd had to lift her up to hug him, it had always been one of his favorite parts of his day. "How was your date?"

"It wasn't really a date," she said. "We mostly just walked around town and talked."

"Walked around town?"

"It's snowing, Daddy. Didn't you and Mom ever just go for a walk when it was snowing?"

They had. He was going to say something about school, when she asked, "Do you think it'd be okay to invite the Davenports over for Thanksgiving dinner?"

"I think your mother was planning on something quiet."

"I'll ask her in the morning," she said. She yawned.

"Tired?" he asked.

"Yes." She walked toward him, and he put the book down on the table and stood. She wrapped her arms around him and held him tight. "Good night, Daddy."

"Good night, Honey." He smelled her hair. Mostly he was checking to see if it smelled like cigarettes, but all he smelled was shampoo. He took a moment to enjoy the hug. They had gotten shorter lately and he wasn't going to wait until she let go first. She kissed his cheek and headed for the stairs.

Chapter 5

Harry Vaughn tended to talk with his hands. In board meetings, if he was making a speech, he would motion with his hand in a rolling motion, a sort of on-and-on-so-on-and-so-forth move. If he was making a point, he would poke the tabletop hard, as if he was trying to do some sort of amazing martial arts trick to impress the volunteers who ran the church. If he was angry, he would flail his arms about wildly, with no rhyme or reason or connection with what he was saying.

Reverend Tumbler knew all of Harry Vaughn's body language. Tumbler was a controlling man who didn't like change. As Reverend Tumbler approached the church building, he saw Harry waving his arms wildly as he talked to the sheriff. Tumbler thought to himself, "Nobody has seen me yet. I could just turn around and go back to my car and ..."

"Reverend Tumbler!" Harry called out.

Tumbler took a deep breath and pushed aside the strong urge to utter what his mother used to call "kitchen language." Sheriff Forbes, who had simply been standing there letting Harry rant and rave, turned to see him come closer. Deputy Royce was sectioning off the church's front lawn with bright yellow police ribbon. "Somebody broke in," Reverend Tumbler thought, "Maybe someone trashed the sanctuary. Maybe someone trashed my office. Maybe someone broke in and stole the Ladies Quilting Circle's Prize Quilt that they were going to raffle off the Sunday before Thanksgiving."

Tumbler liked that quilt. It had been sewn by a group of matronly women of the church, who had each started at a different corner and had simply assumed the other three would follow her lead with colors and patterns. The result was exactly what you'd expect when you started out on a journey without any clue about where you would end up. Tumbler loved it. They were having trouble selling the raffle tickets, though. Tumbler had bought a dozen.

Reverend Tumbler had no idea what Harry's problem was this time, but—knowing Harry—it was entirely possible the commotion was over someone letting their dog dump on the church lawn. Harry was probably insisting on the yellow tape and waiting for Deputy Royce to take a plaster print of the offending pile.

Harry looked up as Reverend Tumbler got closer. "Finally!" he said, exasperated, as if he had been waiting since Moses was a toddler. "We've been trying to reach you for hours," Harry said. "Just look!"

Harry gestured sweepingly towards the lawn. Rev. Tumbler looked. He stared for the longest time, and for the life of him he could not see anything out of the ordinary. Tumbler looked to the sheriff for help.

"I've got Deputy Royce on it," the sheriff said, shaking the minister's gloved hand.

"That's not enough!" Harry shouted.

Reverend Tumbler looked at the lawn again and again, hoping he wasn't going to seem as stupid as he felt. Finally he turned back to Harry Vaughn and asked, "What's the problem?"

Harry gestured toward the lawn again, and made a face he had seen on Vaughn's teenage daughter. The look said, "Well, duh."

Reverend Tumbler put his hands in his pockets. He said, "Harry, I was working late. I haven't had my coffee yet today. Since I seem to be missing the obvious this morning, I would really appreciate it if you could possibly fill me in on what's got you so upset."

Harry turned to the sheriff, as if to say, "See what I have to deal with?"

He turned back toward the minister and said, "Reverend, we were robbed!"

He pointed to the spot where the shepherds had once stood. "Somebody took the shepherds."

Tumbler looked again. Indeed, the life-sized

Nativity was now shepherdless. The minister turned toward the sheriff.

"Probably kids," the sheriff said. "I'll look around. Usually, when this sort of thing happens, the things just get moved someplace the kids think is funny. About ten years ago, Mrs. Foster had the Virgin Mary stolen from right in front of her house. It was returned six years later."

Harry Vaughn said, "Six years?" He was envisioning having to wait that long for the shepherds to return.

"Don't think you'll have to wait that long," the sheriff said. "My guess is that you'll find the shepherds later today on top of the high school or at the McDonald's drive-through."

"Probably hungry," Tumbler said. The sheriff smiled.

"What about prints?" Harry asked, angry that the minister was not as upset as he was.

The sheriff said, "My guess is that any prints we might find would be on the shepherd statues—and since they aren't here…"

"Footprints, then," Harry said. "Take some plaster casts or something."

"Any footprints would have melted with the snow, and I've got our top detective working on finding anything someone might have left behind by accident."

Harry turned and looked at Deputy Royce, who was slowly walking through the lawn examining the ground.

Harry rolled his eyes. "Is that it?"

"Pretty much every man we've got," Forbes said. "Town council voted us down on the budget." Forbes said this because he knew Harry was one of the dissenting votes on the town council. "I've been authorized to deputize citizens in case of emergency. I'm not sure this qualifies."

The message was not subtle, nor was it meant to be. Harry Vaughn was not a stupid man, nor was he a forgetful one. He would remember this. At some point, Deputy Royce might want a promotion, or Forbes might find himself in some sort of bind and he would ask the council for help, and Harry Vaughn had already made up his mind that he wasn't going to give it to him.

Harry drifted away from Forbes and the pastor and walked toward Deputy Royce. He bent low and stepped under the tape that said "CRIME SCENE."

The sheriff watched him go. "Tightly wound," he said.

"The man is a bedspring," Tumbler said. The two men exchanged a knowing look, as Harry Vaughn made his way toward Deputy Royce.

Harry looked back over his shoulder, to make sure he was out of earshot of the pair, and asked, "Any thoughts, Deputy?"

"The sheriff will have a report for you soon," Royce said.

Harry took a small step closer and waited for Deputy Royce to look up at him from under the brim of his hat. Harry spoke quietly. "I know what the sheriff is going to say." Then, even quieter: "I'm asking what you think."

Deputy Royce studied Harry Vaughn's face for a moment, checking to see whether he was making fun of him or being serious. "I think it was kids," the deputy said. "It's a bigger problem than most people know. Most folks don't lock their cars or their front doors, and one of these days one of these kids who's into the drugs are going to come knocking on their door with a knife or a shotgun."

"You think this was drug-related?" Harry Vaughn asked. He made his face full of parental concern. He didn't think for a moment that the theft was drug related—but he thought that, if he could get Deputy Royce to trust him, he would have an ally on the town police force. On a force of two full-time people and one part-time, that was almost 50%.

Rev. Tumbler and Sheriff Forbes watched Harry and Royce speaking quietly. "That can't be good," Forbes said.

"The deputy is an eager young man, is he?" Tumbler asked.

"The deputy thinks he's better than his current position as the deputy in a small town," Forbes said. "He probably is. He has good instincts and the drive, but he has a tendency to see bigger things than may be there."

Tumbler nodded.

"My guess, Reverend," Forbes said, "is that in about a day or two we'll see your missing shepherds on top of the coffee shop. We'll bring them down and make sure they find their way home."

Tumbler held out his hand. "Thank you, Sheriff."

Forbes, also a widower, shook it. For just a moment there was a link between them. Tumbler looked deep into the sheriff's eyes and saw the sympathy. No, it wasn't sympathy. It was that link between two people who have each lost a family member. Forbes' eighteen-year-old son had died of an overdose, about six months before Tumbler's wife and son were killed by a drunk driver. Soon after, the grief ripped his marriage apart and he found himself entirely alone.

After seeking comfort in a bottle and finding none, Forbes had landed one day in Tumbler's office and fallen apart on his mini-sofa. He had cried a full five minutes before Tumbler had offered any sort of solace. Forbes was a fixture on that sofa, every Friday, for about seven weeks. He always brought the coffee; Tumbler brought the shoulder.

Sheriff Forbes was the one who'd had to knock on Reverend Tumbler's door and tell him that his wife and baby son were in a car that was barely recognizable as a vehicle, at the bottom of Shepherd's Pass. The drunk driver who had slammed into the back of the minivan had gone over the embankment after them, and had landed upside down on top of them. At first, the firemen weren't aware there was a second car involved.

Both Mrs. Tumbler and her son Joey had been killed instantly. (Forbes had been told by the EMS that the baby had probably survived for a half-hour or so after the crash, but Forbes saw no need to tell the minister that.)

It had been a relationship of two men who were well acquainted with loss: a relationship that had been born out of grief, and that had slowly dissolved when they came to the realization that grief was all that linked them together.

After the accident, Reverend Tumbler had slipped into a dark well of despair. Some had thought he would move away from Summer Park, but he didn't. For three months, Mary Jane practically ran the church. Tumbler sat in his office and was happy to let things be run for him. His sermons were filled with sad imagery, and his messages were on redemption, sanctification, and sin. The only one who took to these messages was Harry Vaughn, who had often thought that Tumbler's sermons lacked any sort of "wake-'em-up" aspect.

One summer night about five months after the accident, Tumbler was lying in his bed, feeling the breeze that came in through the screen window. He suddenly got it into his head to sleep out on the roof. He had often slept on the roof when he was in college and had always woken refreshed. He thought the summer air would do him good.

Carrying his blanket and pillow, he slipped through the window and stretched out with his body leaning back vertically against the roof.

The night was clear. There were no clouds. Tumbler lay there and contemplated the vastness of the heavens before him and found himself feeling very small and lonely.

He was awakened by dampness in his PJs. When he opened his eyes, he was looking at the morning sky. He was startled to see the roof above him as well. The dampness came from the dewy grass in which he lay. He lay there silently taking a sort of bodily inventory. "Perhaps I've broken both legs," he thought, "and I don't feel it because I've also broken my spine and I'm paralyzed."

He moved one leg and then the other. He lifted his hand, so that he could see his own fingers. He wiggled them. Yes, they seemed to work as well. He rolled his head from side to side and found that nothing on his body anywhere seemed to be broken or even bruised.

He knew for certain that, somewhere in the night, he had fallen asleep and rolled off the roof, pillow and all. Staring at the morning sky, he tried to see if he could remember a dream in which angels of God gently lowered him to the grass—but there was no such memory. He stood, expecting to feel aches and pains, but instead felt better than he had in a long time.

"Having a camp-out, Pastor?" Tumbler turned to see the papergirl staring at him.

"Oh, I was, uh…I guess I…. Yeah, Jenny. I was having a camp-out. Seemed like a nice night."

Jenny handed the moist pastor his morning paper and pedaled off. To the best of Tumbler's knowledge the papergirl never mentioned it to anyone.

The pastor made his way into the house, put on a pot of coffee, and headed for the shower. While

washing the grass from his hair, he suddenly realized something very clearly. He didn't hear it in his
head like a voice. It wasn't even an original idea. It
was just a very clear realization that he would not
have believed six weeks before. He thought to himself: "Life goes on."

"Not very original, but very true." Tumbler
thought as he drove to work. He thought about
putting it on a bumper sticker or a T-shirt, but he
knew he would then be sure to see it written in
needlepoint, framed, and wrapped up in Christmas
wrapping paper when the gift-giving season rolled
around again. Probably it would be done by Mrs.
O'Donnell. She was a master of the art of needlepoint— but if he had to find a place for one more
throw pillow or framed masterpiece, he would have
to ask for an addition on the church to store
unwanted gifts. So the message "Life goes on"
remained solely inside his head.

The first thing he had done upon arriving in his
office had been to open the window and shades,
something that he could not recall doing since he
had first come there. Sunlight and fresh air
enveloped the stale room, and Tumbler went to the
custodian's closet and spent the morning cleaning
and vacuuming. He then crafted a sermon that was
so full of love and joy that his dwindling congregation promptly went out and told everyone that the
old Reverend Tumbler was back. Reverend
Tumbler himself thought of it more as the arrival of
a "new-and-improved" Rev. Tumbler, but he would
take what he could get.

The only thing that still got to him was the Christmas season. His missed his wife and baby more at this time of year. The hassles of trying to make everyone else have a perfect Christmas had no compensating rewards. He had no one to hold his hand. He had no reason to look forward to going home. His wife had always been there to rub his shoulders and to listen to his ranting and raving about the church. The most joyous time of year for most Christians is the worst time of year for those who actually work for the being who set up the first Christmas. Each year, at Christmas time, seemed worse than the last. Tumbler was beginning to feel like the Grinch. There was one small part of him that half hoped the rest of the Nativity would vanish along with the shepherds.

"The shepherds heard the message and ignored it," Tumbler thought. "They just decided to stick around with the sheep. That would have made things a little different. At the very least, it would have made casting the Christmas pageant harder. One Joseph, three wise men, and every other boy would have to be an angel." The pastor smiled and watched the sheriff walk toward the station. He could see the sheriff's office from the front lawn of the church, yet Deputy Royce still chose to drive the police car and run the lights.

As the car passed him by, Forbes simply hung his head and looked at his feet. "What would happen," Reverend Tumbler wondered to himself, "if we all just suddenly decided to keep Christmas in our hearts and not on our front lawns?"

"You know, Reverend," Harry Vaughn said, "I'm thinking that if you preach a sermon on 'Thou shalt not steal,' maybe the ones who took it will feel guilty and put it back."

"You think it was a member of our congregation?" Tumbler asked Harry.

"You never know, Reverend. Could be right under your nose."

❄ ❄ ❄

Poison stood at his locker, staring at the stack of books, trying to remember which class he was going to.

"Hey, Angel Boy," Doreen said, coming up behind him. She leaned against the row of lockers and studied him. He looked awful.

"What period is this?" Poison asked.

"You don't even know what period it is? Didn't you get any sleep?"

Poison pulled the science book from the top of the stack, but something about it looked "fresh" somehow, as if maybe he had just come from science, which meant he needed his math book.

"It's third period. You have algebra," Doreen said. "You're not going to be worth much, are you? I hope you don't have a test."

Poison didn't remember if he did or didn't. He didn't think so. He stood looking at Doreen, who seemed to be waiting for him to say something. "New sweater?" He asked. The soft fuzzy sweater did look new to him.

"Nice try."

"Earrings?"

"If you are going to pull this stunt off, you're going to have to find a way to get some sleep. What did you do? Sneak out of the house and work all night?"

Poison shook his head. "I got some sleep." Which was true: he'd crawled back through his bedroom window and been asleep for a full twenty minutes before his alarm went off. Poison vaguely remembered throwing the alarm clock, but he didn't remember hearing it hit the wall or the floor. He wondered where it was. He looked back up at the books in his locker.

"Algebra," Doreen said.

"Thanks. New colored contacts?"

"You're pathetic."

"You mean your eyes are naturally that green?"

She rolled her eyes—which were indeed "naturally that green"—and kissed him on the cheek. He felt the warmth of her lips even as she walked away from him. He wondered how long it would last. He didn't dare reach up and touch it, for fear it might go away.

He turned back toward his locker and stared at the books again. The "tardy" bell rang as he grabbed the science book and headed to the class he had just come from.

Chapter 6

Poison drove the book van through the crowded streets—well, at least as crowded as streets can get in Summer Park. Most days, a person could stop in the middle of the street and not have anyone blow their horn at them. This is partly because most folks in Summer Park are friendly and would decide you had a good reason for stopping in the middle of the street, and partly because, well, how long would a person want to stand in the middle of the street in November? It was snowing just enough for Poison to turn on the windshield wipers. There was no one standing in the road.

Poison was on his way to pick up Doreen. He had invited her to his house for supper. It was Friday night: he was supposed to go pick up a pizza and come home. At the last minute, he'd asked his mother if he could pick up Doreen too. She'd said "Sure." Brenda liked Doreen. She was fun, but she had a good head on her shoulders. She was good for Poison.

Poison was looking forward to showing Doreen the progress he had made on the shepherds. It was his plan to get the shepherds done in the next day or two, and then switch them out with the wise men.

He had heard about the "prank" or "theft" in school: whether it was a "theft" or a "prank" depended on whom you asked.

The last time a senior had pulled something stupid had been the year Poison was in the 8th grade. Someone had tried to steal the "Big Boy" statue from in front of the restaurant. Finding it too heavy to drag out once it had been knocked it over, the thief had simply left it in the parking lot. Poison knew who it was. Pretty much everyone in Summer Park High School knew who it was, but no one said anything.

Mr. Hawthorne, the principal, had called a special assembly to ask anyone with information to come forward. He had said that senseless acts of vandalism would not be tolerated. Mr. Hawthorne ate at Big Boy at least three times a week, and the manager claimed that someone had seen teenagers skulking around the statue earlier that day. Since the Big Boy incident, though, the town of Summer Park had been relatively safe from skulking teenagers.

Poison pulled the van into Doreen's driveway. She was out the door and down the steps before he stopped the car. Her father stood in the doorway, watching her go.

"How's the assignment going, Angel Boy?"

Doreen asked as she climbed into the passenger seat.

"I'm done with the shepherds."

"You're kidding. That was quick. Wave to my father."

Poison waved. Ted Hudson did not move. "Maybe he can't see me," Poison thought. "Maybe it's too dark and the only reason I see him is because it's light in the house."

Ted Hudson took a step backward and closed the door. Poison looked at Doreen. "What'd I do now?"

"You didn't come up to the door to get me."

"I didn't get a chance. You came out as soon as I pulled up."

"Doesn't matter." Doreen said. "As far as my father is concerned you should have been out of the car before you pulled up—and laid your coat on the ground so I wouldn't have to step in the snow."

"If I got out of the van before I pulled up, how would I get it stopped?"

"Your mistake is that you're thinking in a logical manner," Doreen said. "This is father-thinking. Logic is not a prerequisite. You have a penis. That's the only fact on his mind."

Poison did his best not to drive off the road. "I'm not sure what that has to do with it."

"You have a penis, and you are picking up his daughter in a moving vehicle," Doreen said, as if it were plain and simple.

"These are two things I have very little control over."

Doreen looked at him. He saw her brown eyes smiling.

"I mean," he said, "that I have no control over whether or not I have a penis, and I have no choice but to pick you up—since it is the only way in which I can take you to my parents' nice safe home for pizza—which we still have to pick up, by the way."

She smiled at him again. "I think my father would prefer that you had neither."

"I'm going to change the subject now," Poison ventured.

"Go for it."

"I ordered pizza from Benny's."

"Benny's is good."

"You and I and my mother will share one. My dad likes fish and pineapple, so he gets his own."

"I hate anchovies," Doreen said. She crinkled her nose. Poison thought it looked adorable. He made a mental note to say the word "anchovies" every time they discussed pizza, so he could see that nose crinkle again. He thought for a moment about what it would be like to watch your only daughter get into a van with someone you didn't like or trust all that much. He wondered if Ted Hudson owned a gun.

Doreen's father rarely used human logic when he thought of his daughter dating. Father-logic was perfectly okay for him. It didn't matter if it made no sense to his daughter. She was just like her mother, and her mother didn't see the logic in his logic either.

Ted Hudson referred to Poison as "that boy" from "that family" in all conversations. Doreen wondered if her father was going to say "that grandchild" if she and Poison ever decided to get married—which, she had assured her father, was not even a topic of discussion. Her father had met Poison more than a dozen times, and each time Poison had been polite and courteous and gentlemanly. Poison had once had her mother as an art teacher. Her mother had vouched for him, saying he was a good boy.

Doreen looked at Poison. It was getting dark early, and he looked pale in the light of the dashboard.

"Have you gotten any sleep?"

"Some," he said.

"I can help, you know. I'm not an artist, but I can do a coat of primer or something."

"I was going to ask you," Poison said. "At the rate I'm going, I'm not sure I'll be able to finish before Christmas. I was thinking that maybe after supper you could help me with some of it."

"You said the shepherds are done."

"Almost," he explained. "They both need a coat of lacquer. I made a mold and a plaster cast of the shepherd's face that I can use on the wise man. The face needs to be painted. If I can get some of this done, I can put those pieces back in a few days and take the wise men."

"There was a police car in front of the church," Doreen said.

"I heard. Must be the biggest crime of the last fifty years."

"What do you think people will say when they see the shepherds come back and the Wise Men disappear?"

"Who knows?" Poison said. "I'm hoping they quit thinking of it as a crime: there's no stealing. We're putting them back. I'm hoping for urban legend status. Mostly I just want to do this for the Reverend Tumbler. I saw him the other day. It's like he can't get a break. Maybe this will be like a...uh..." He searched for the word.

"Scrooge event?" Doreen offered.

"Like that. But he's not a Scrooge to begin with, so that's not it."

"I know what you mean, anyway," Doreen said. She adjusted the heater vent to blow on her feet. Poison reached over and turned the heat up.

"So your dad likes fish and pineapple. What does your mom like on her pizza?" Doreen asked.

"If dad is working late, then she gets chicken and tomatoes. Other than that, she's pretty traditional and goes with pepperoni. Come over after Thanksgiving, and you can have my mother's famous turkey quesadillas."

She looked at him without saying anything.

"They're better than they sound. Does your family do traditional Thanksgiving or more of an island theme?"

"An island theme?"

"I mean, do you eat food from the Bahamas or American food?"

"We always went to my grandfather's house. My mom would take this really spicy vegetable dish her mother taught her to make. Everybody loves it, and then complains about it afterward. Like it's never Aunt Margaret's oyster stuffing, or the sweet potatoes, it's always my mother's dish."

"Are you going back this year?"

"No," she said—but before he could ask why, she changed the subject. "I want to see the shepherds. Can we do that when we get there, or do we have to go right in?"

"You can see them. Mom and Dad still think I'm working on some mystery Christmas present."

"Question," Doreen said.

"Shoot."

"If it's going to take you until Christmas to finish the Nativity, what are you going to give your parents for a gift?"

"I'm working on that," Poison said. The truth was that he had no idea. The whole truth was that he was hoping the angel would cut him some slack and conjure something out of thin air for him to wrap up the day before Christmas. The problem was he still hadn't seen Bez-A-Lel, or any other angel, since being given the assignment. He turned the van onto his street and yawned. He inhaled deeply and smelled the perfume that he had picked out for Doreen for her last birthday.

❊ ❊ ❊

Doreen finished her third slice of pizza and leaned back in her chair. "Oh, my, that was wonderful. Thank you for inviting me, Mrs. Davenport."

"Any time, Doreen," Poison's mom said. She looked at him over the rim of her glasses.

"You sure you don't want to try some fish and pineapple?" Snake asked her. He was grinning. Doreen crinkled her nose, and now Poison was grinning.

"No, thank you," Doreen said. "I hear you are an expert with turkey leftovers, Mrs. Davenport."

"Brenda is going to write a cookbook on what to do with Thanksgiving leftovers," Snake said.

Doreen smiled. "I heard about the turkey quesadillas."

Snake said, "We've done casseroles, soups, tacos, and..."

"And that caramel turkey pie was a winner." Poison said. It was supposed to be funny, but everyone just looked at him.

Brenda asked, "Doreen, does your family have plans for Thanksgiving?"

"Not really. We used to go to my grandfather's house, but he died last January."

"Oh, I'm sorry." Brenda said.

"Thanks." Doreen answered. "My dad's brother and sister both decided to spend Thanksgiving with the other families....I mean their in-laws...do you know what I mean?"

Brenda nodded.

"So," Doreen said, "since my mother's family is in the Bahamas, it looks as if it will be just us." She stood up quickly, as if she had said too much. "I'll help with the table."

"Thank you," Brenda said, "but Poison can do it by himself."

Poison stood and began to clear the table. "I like this," Doreen said.

"Train 'em young," Brenda said, "and they'll keep you happy forever."

"Mom!" Poison groaned.

Brenda smiled. "Doreen, would you like to see pictures of Poison when he was a baby?"

"Moooooooooom!" Poison said again—turning it into a three-syllable word.

"I'd love to," Doreen said. Without another word, the two of them stood and went into the other room.

"Dad—" Poison pleaded with his father.

"Don't look at me," Snake shot back. He stood and helped Poison clear the table. The two men loaded the dishwasher and put the food away. Poison tried as hard as he could to ignore the giggles from the other room. Suddenly he heard an "Ohhhhhhhhhhhhhhhhhhhh," followed by an extended laugh. Poison looked at his dad.

"I think they found the one of you in the biker jacket with your little butt peeking out," Snake grinned.

Poison hung his head and put the leftover pizza in the refrigerator.

After a while, the two of them returned to the kitchen. Poison was trying hard not to look at Doreen who was giving him the I-saw-your-baby-butt-picture look. Doreen took pity on him, and tried not to embarrass him by saying any of the thousand comments that were in her mind. "C'mon, Angel Boy, you said you'd show me what you were making for your parents' Christmas present."

"You want to see it?" Poison asked.

Snake looked at Poison and silently mouthed, "Angel Boy?"

Poison gave his father a look that pleaded, "My God, Dad, please! Haven't I suffered enough?"

"Sorry," Snake said.

"Show me," Doreen said, staring at him with her eyes wide, asking with them, "Did I just screw up?"

Poison grabbed his coat from the hook by the door, helped Doreen on with her own, and they went out the door holding hands. Brenda stood at the kitchen window and watched the light come on in the garage. Snake said, "Did you see him help her on with her coat?"

"Yesterday I saw him open the car door for her. It wasn't a put-on. He wasn't even thinking about it—he just did it."

"We raised a gentleman." Snake held up his hand and Brenda gave him a soft high-five. They both stood there together looking out the window at the garage. "I'm guessing the gentleman would not want us watching the garage where he's working on a Christmas present for us."

"Our seventeen-year-old just went into a dimly lit garage with his girlfriend, and they are alone," Brenda said. "Do you think he's going to show her some Christmas present?"

"Then what else would he....oh," Snake said. He

and Brenda both turned away from the window. Brenda sat at the table, and Snake pulled two coffee cups from the cupboard and filled them. "How long do you think we should allow them to be alone out there?"

"Well," Brenda said, "My guess is he'll be back in about fifteen minutes to get a schoolbook of some kind and tell us that Doreen is going to drill him on history facts while he works, so it's like studying."

"You think the whole gift thing is just a ruse for a make-out place?"

"Sooner or later, he's going to have to cough up a present that looks like he's spent weeks on it," Brenda said. "I'm thinking our 'Angel Boy' is actually working on something."

Snake picked up the evening paper and sipped his coffee. "Did you see this?" he said. "Someone stole part of the Nativity scene from the church downtown."

"I saw the police tape around the yard."

"Our good friend deputy Royce is treating it like a major crime wave."

"Royce needs to get a life."

When Snake and Brenda had first moved to town and lived above the bookstore with Poison, Snake had been pulled over by Deputy Royce for driving his motorcycle without a helmet. The next week, he had been pulled over for driving his motorcycle over the speed limit in a school zone. Both times, Deputy Royce had given him a lecture about what a nice quiet town Summer Park was and how they didn't want any undesirable element coming in.

The third time he was pulled over, Poison had been in the sidecar and Deputy Royce gave him a ticket for transporting a child without a legal, secure car seat. Snake had taken his complaint to the sheriff—who decided that, having no other vehicle, Snake could take Poison around in the car seat until the bookstore started to make enough money to buy a car. Sheriff Forbes tore up the helmet ticket and the safety-seat ticket, but let the speeding-in-a-school-zone citation stand. Snake agreed and paid the fine, but spent the next several years with Deputy Royce following behind him every time he went through the school zone.

"The whole Nativity, or just part of it?" Brenda asked.

"Just the shepherds."

"That's too bad."

"Who would take life-sized plaster shepherds off a church lawn?" Snake asked.

"Who would climb up the side of a Catholic Church to put a Harley Davidson shirt on the Jesus statue?"

"Oh. Okay, never mind."

❄   ❄   ❄

In the garage, the face of one of the shepherds stared up at Doreen from a sheet of newspaper. It was copied perfectly from a mold that Poison had made off of one of the two shepherds standing by the workbench.

"It's perfect," said Doreen. "How are you going to attach it to the wise man?"

"I bought a fiberglass patch kit. I had it left over from the time I backed out of the garage without opening the door."

Doreen smiled. She remembered that: he'd been grounded for two months. She put her hand over her mouth to keep from giggling.

"Thanks," Poison said, knowing what she was thinking. "I'm pretty sure I can make it work. Do you want to put a coat of primer on the face?"

"Sure." Doreen walked over to where Poison was painting a second coat of lacquer on one of the shepherd statues. She stared a moment at the work Poison had done. The shepherd had once looked as if it had been painted by a seven-year-old—none of the colors blending. All the pieces, in fact, had looked like something out of a three-dimensional version of a coloring book.

She remembered the time someone had given the statue of Mary a thick coat of blue eye shadow to match her blue robe. Jokes had been made in town about how the Virgin Mary didn't look all that virginal.

Now she studied the way Poison had restored the shepherds. He had made the robes look like real fabric. The shepherds now had different hair colors; previously they would have passed for identical twins.

Poison had taken a great deal of time to work on

the eyes, probably hours. They were dark and deep. One of the shepherds was looking at the ground. The other was gazing away, as if he were wondering about something. She was amazed at the character that each figure had. One even looked older than the other.

"I have one question," Doreen said, "and I don't want you to think any less of me for asking; I just want to ask. Okay?"

Poison continued to paint the clear finish on the back of the second shepherd's head. "Okay."

"The shepherds are a lot...well...darker than they were. I mean, before they were pretty white. Now they're darker."

"Now they look as if they're from the Middle East." Poison said. "It's more accurate."

"I'm all for accuracy. But do you think this could cause a problem down the road?"

"Right now, I'm more worried about putting these back and getting the wise men out of there without getting caught."

"How long will it take the lacquer to dry?'

"Tomorrow. I want to see if I can still work on that face tonight. There's a hair dryer on the tool bench. Can you plug that in and see if you can dry that primer on the face? Set it on Cool."

"I can do that. Do you want to go get your history book from the house so it will look like we're studying?"

"Good idea." He set down the brush and can of lacquer, and left her alone to go get his history book.

❋ ❋ ❋

Ted Hudson was reading the paper when the phone rang. Ted had a rule about phones. He did not answer them at home. He answered them all day at work, and he didn't think it was too much to ask not to be bothered by the damn things after supper. He hated telemarketers, and often told them to do things that were physically impossible. Besides, most of the calls were for his wife or his daughter. He let it ring.

Iza Hudson came into the room, drying her hands with a dishtowel. As she passed her husband reading, she snapped the towel quickly—just missing his ear—and knocked the newspaper out of his hands. He rolled his eyes, picked it back up, and started reading again.

"'Ello?"

"Iza? This is Brenda Davenport. Poison's mom? We've met a few times."

"Ohhhhhh, yes." Iza said. "Pretty lady in de bookstore. How are you?"

"Better, now that I've been called 'pretty lady,'" Brenda said.

"Is somt'ing wrong?" Iza asked

"No, no, no. Doreen and Poison are studying. I was just talking to Doreen, and she mentioned that you folks didn't have any plans for Thanksgiving..."

Chapter 7

Ted Hudson stood in his kitchen and inhaled deeply. He loved the smell of a humming kitchen. When he had been very young, his mother had set him on a stool in the middle of the room and let him taste and smell things as she cooked. It was a treasured memory. In front of him was the oven where the turkey was fast becoming a thing of beauty. Behind him he smelled gingerbread cookies. He had smelled these when he woke up. He walked into the kitchen still rubbing his eyes. His wife, who looked as if she was going to burst with joy, handed him a cookie right off the cookie sheet. He touched it gingerly and blew on it to cool it off.

"Coffee is in de pot," Iza said. She was practically dancing. As much as Ted Hudson was dreading this day, he was enjoying seeing his wife glow this way. When she was happy, she would be a little more lax on the "no bad foods" rule.

Doreen was at the sink washing the Pilgrim salt

and pepper shakers that came out of the closet once a year on Thanksgiving. He could hear the Macy's Parade on the television in the other room.

He poured himself a cup of coffee and said, "Explain to me again why we're having this little shindig here, when we were the ones who were invited."

"Poison's house isn't that big. We have a dining room and a huge TV screen so you can watch football."

"Don't butter me up, girl." He was smiling. The cookies were wonderful and made him feel happy.

"I want to be havin' de big dinner here," Iza said. "Since I been married to you I don' ever make a turkey. Your sister, she always make de turkey, and dis year dey all goin' someplace else...I git to make de turkey." She kissed him. He kissed her back.

"What are our guests bringing?"

"I tol' her to bring de pies," Iza said, looking at him for his reaction.

"You're not making pies?"

"I make de turkey," she said, "and de gravy, and de potatoes, and de stuffing, and all de stuff dat go with de birdy. Poison mom, she make de breads, de vegetables, and de pies."

"Poison's mom is a great cook, Daddy," Doreen said. She was calling him "Daddy." She did that when she was trying to keep him happy.

He sipped his coffee. He hoped that "that boy's" mom made a good pie. He also hoped she made several.

"Go get a shower," Iza said. "You wearin' a tie today."

"I'm not wearing a tie."

"You wearin' a tie today. My baby bringin' over da boy she like, and da boy bringin' his family, and it's T'anksgivin'. So, you wearing a tie, or you don' get any more of my cookies."

Ted Hudson turned and poured a second cup of coffee, as he slyly grabbed another cookie and held his hand very casually down by his side. She would never know. He wandered toward the bedroom. He said, "I'll think about it."

Iza, who had seen him take the cookie, said "Wear da one wit de red stripes."

Poison was tying his tie for the third time. He thought, "My father is meeting my girlfriend's father."

He untied the tie and tried again. He thought, "My mother is going to be spending time with my girlfriend's mother."

The skinny end of his tie poked out of the bottom and mocked him. He pulled it off his neck and tossed it at the mirror.

His father came into the room. Snake was wearing a starched white shirt that looked brand-new. His collar was buttoned, and he wore a tie that looked like it had been made from a 1950s Hawaiian shirt. "Ties are our friends," Snake said.

"Ties are symbols of slavery to corporate consumerism," Poison retorted.

Snake draped the tie around his son's neck. "Ties make us look like adults."

"Ties cut off circulation to the brain, thereby stifling creativity, thus creating corporate drones."

Snake carefully slid the knot up the tie, tucked it into his son's collar, and formed a perfect Windsor. "Ties impress women, and make us look mature and handsome in their eyes."

"Ties are our friends," Poison sighed.

Brenda sped past the doorway of Poison's bedroom. She was barefoot and was trying to fasten an earring as she ran. She yelled "Burning muffins!" as she ran by.

"Wasn't The Burning Muffins another of your favorite bands?" Poison asked his father.

"You're a funny guy. I already pulled the muffins from the oven. They are unburned."

"Thaaaaaaaaank Yoooooooooou!" Brenda sang from the kitchen.

She had opened the oven. The smell of the four pies wafted its way to the stairs. Snake inhaled deeply. "Your mother makes good pie."

He started for the door and then turned around. "Do you have any instructions for me?"

"Excuse me?" Poison asked.

"Are there subjects I should avoid? Mannerisms that I don't want to share, habits that are disgusting, is there anything about my person that could embarrass you on this day when I meet your girlfriend's parents?"

Poison, touched by the sentiment, suddenly realized that perhaps his father was more of a kindred spirit than he'd thought. Snake had not made a good impression on his own girlfriend's father. When they had married, Brenda's father had not attended. When Poison had been born, Brenda had received a check for a thousand dollars to be used toward college.

Poison thought a lot over the years about what his parents had gone through to be together. He thought mostly about what his mother had given up. It had only recently occurred to him what his own father might have felt.

Poison came over and hugged his dad. They didn't let go after the usual five-seconds-with-a-back-slap ending. They held the embrace until Poison said, "Just keep me from saying something stupid."

Snake smiled and released his son. "Did I ever tell you the last thing I said to your grandfather as we walked out the door?"

"No."

"Good." Snake turned and went down the stairs. "We'll be leaving soon. I'm going to need your help loading the bench seat into the book van."

❋   ❋   ❋

Doreen stood at the mirror in the dining room, watching the mirror image of the Macy's Parade. She didn't remember it being such a commercial thing when she was younger. When she was younger, it had been part of the magic of the holidays. She longed to someday show up in New York at 4 o'clock in the morning, holding a cup of coffee and a thermos full of refills. It would be cold when she went. She would have on a really cute scarf and hat. She would be wearing really big mittens, but she would only need one because the other would be wrapped around Poison's hand and hiding in his coat pocket. She had imagined this before. In her daydream, Poison was older. His hair was shorter and he was wearing glasses instead of contacts: really nice glasses that made him look really smart. There would be lots and lots of people around, but they would still find a spot near the front. They would hold hands. They would kiss occasionally. He would be taller, so he could see over the crowd and know which balloons were coming next.

Doreen seemed to remember when none of the balloons had actually been commercials for parade sponsors. She remembered when Big Bird had been just Big Bird and hadn't worn a sweater with someone's logo on it. Her father had told her that Macy's used to have a Superman balloon. It had been his favorite but he hadn't seen it in years. She had trouble imagining her father liking Superman. She remembered a float based on the book *The Hobbit*. It had been there the year she had read the book for the first time. There had been a dragon on the top with long red wings. She remembered being fascinated.

Doreen brushed where she had just curled, and started a second row. She looked at the reflection, and wondered why there was a giant chili pepper driving down the street and then read the word "Chili's" (actually "s'ilihC") on the side. "Cause everybody thinks of hot chili peppers on Thanksgiving," she thought.

She studied her own reflection in the mirror. She never saw her own face in her dreams of going to New York or some other big city. But she was always with Poison, and he was always older in her dreams, so she assumed she was older in them too.

She didn't think it was a premonition but she hoped it was.

She pulled the curling iron out of her hair and set it on the table. As she brushed her hair, staring at her reflection, she saw her mother come up behind her and hug her from behind.

"My baby, having de happy T'anksgivin'?"

"Yes, Mom," Doreen said smiling. She waited a moment, and then asked, "Is Daddy going to be good?"

"Your daddy jes' bein' a daddy," Iza said. She was talking to her daughter's face in the mirror. "Yo daddy, he see somet'ing dat have a penis, an' he be holdin' hands wit' 'is only baby girl. So, yo daddy havin' a little trouble."

Doreen opened her mouth, shocked. She had never heard her mother say...that word.

"Don' be lookin' at me.' Iza says. "No man like to see his daughter wit' a boy. He wan' sometin' bad to happ'n so he can jump in an' be yo' hero. So he prob'ly lookin' for sometin' to complain 'bout."

"You can make him be nice, right?" Doreen

asked. She was looking at how much her mother's eyes looked like her own.

Iza leaned her chin on her daughter's shoulders and said, "You like dis boy, don' you?"

Doreen stopped brushing, and nodded.

"You t'inkin' dat you love dis boy." She didn't ask it as a question, but Doreen nodded anyway.

"You dreamin' about bein' far away from home and holdin' hands with dis boy and bein' his wife?"

Doreen turned and looked at her mother, face to face. She said, "A lot."

Her mother hugged her and said, "Turn de curlin' iron off and hep me wit' dese' potatoes."

❉ ❉ ❉

Poison sat in the bench seat that he and his father had loaded into the book van. It was going to be hard to get the shepherds and the wise men in here with the bench seat in place. He was going to have to remember to play "the good son" when they got home, and offer to help take it back out. He inhaled deeply, smelling the pies and the muffins. The basket of muffins felt warm on his lap, and he thought about sneaking his hand under the towel and snitching one, but his mother kept looking at him in the rearview mirror. She "looked" at him a lot lately. She'd see him and give one of those my-baby-is-growing-up looks.

There were no windows in the side of the van, so Poison looked out the front windshield. It was starting to snow.

He didn't mind the back of the van so much. As a kid, he had often imagined himself in a tank or an airplane. Once, Tuba had come to their house for Thanksgiving with stories about riding in the Macy's Parade the previous year. Tuba had known a guy who knew a guy who said he could come and ride in one of the floats. As it turned out he was actually riding in the float. He was in the base of the Hobbit float. There was nothing to see, and no windows. The only place to see out was a small square in front of the driver. Tuba said it was still very exciting, even though it felt like he was in a tin can. Poison used to imagine that he was in a Macy's Parade float, and that right above him was a giant red dragon with long red wings.

Chapter 8

If the shepherds had never been returned, most people would have eventually forgotten about the entire incident. Those that remembered would have written it off as a high school prank. Harry Vaughn would have brought it up at every city council meeting for the rest of his life. It would have become one of those small-town unsolved mysteries.

The church would have dipped into the budget, and bought a brand new set of figures, and everyone would have "Ooooooooooooooh"ed and "Ahhhhhhhhhhhhhhhhhh"ed on Christmas Eve.

If the shepherds had simply shown up in their normal state, most people would have forgotten they were ever gone—and Zack Wright would have had to stick to his usual mildly annoying topics. Instead, the shepherds' reappearance-with-makeover gave Zack Wright a story with all his favorite subjects: race, religion, political correctness, and ineffective law enforcement.

If the shepherds had never returned, the Summer Park Police Department would have had to deal with a few mild barbs about "unsolved mysteries," which they could have easily answered with a few comments about lack of funding. Instead, the shepherds' reappearance started a slow burn inside Deputy Royce—who would eventually be fired for excessive violence in the line of duty.

If the shepherds had stayed gone, Reverend Tumbler would have retired early and spent his days on the beach in St. Petersburg, Florida, filling in for vacationing pastors at various retirement villages in the community.

If the shepherds had simply stayed gone...

Poison drove the minivan around the block four times. Each time they passed the police station, Doreen looked in. Each time, she saw Deputy Royce at his desk with his feet up, playing solitaire on the computer. "I feel protected," Doreen said.

"He's there in case a call comes in."

"We could phone something in," Doreen said, "That would make him leave."

"It's also a crime," Poison said. "We get caught doing that, we'd get slammed harder than if we got caught returning the statues."

She settled back down in the seat. "I have to be home in 30 minutes. We have to do this—or not do this."

"If we get caught putting them back, we can always say we found them. It's if we get caught taking the wise men that we're busted."

"You think Officer Rhoid would believe us if we said we're putting them back?"

"No."

"Slow down a second," Doreen said. Poison pressed the brake as they passed the police station. "The man has a hoagy sandwich the size of my arm." She looked over at Poison. "That will take him thirty minutes at least."

They drove around to the other side of the church, where the van couldn't be seen from the police station window where Deputy Royce was enjoying his massive hoagy. Poison stopped and turned off the lights. "There's more snow tonight," he said. "We might leave tracks."

"Not if we try and stay in the same tracks over and over," Doreen said. "Then we can cover them on our way out the last trip."

Poison looked at her in the dim light of the dashboard. "Are you ready?" He knew that she was. Her eyes were bright and clear.

"Let's go," she said.

They opened the doors. Poison lifted the back door. The two shepherds lay there in the back of the van, side by side. They looked different from the way they'd looked when Poison and Doreen had stolen them. To anyone glancing in they would have looked real. That was what Poison had wanted: for the figures to look real enough that folks driving by would look twice to see if the statues had been replaced by live actors.

Poison knew that Reverend Tumbler could see the Nativity from his office window during the day.

He hoped that the minister would feel at least a little better, now that the pieces were starting to return. He hoped that people in town would finally "get it" and stop talking about it.

Careful to stay in one path, Poison and Doreen carried the first shepherd back to the spot where he had been standing only a few days before. Then the second shepherd was replaced, while Doreen kept an eye on the police station window. As far as she could tell, Officer Royce was still sitting and enjoying his enormous sandwich.

The first two wise men were gently lifted off the ground and carried toward the van. Poison and Doreen laid them carefully in the back seats of the minivan. The third wise man was more of a problem. He was kneeling, he was bulky, and he wasn't going to fit into the back.

Doreen said, "He's got to ride up front." Poison looked at her. She said, "I'll ride in the back. I can fold. He can't."

Poison said, "I'm not putting you in the trunk."

"You don't have time to argue," Doreen said. "Rhoid could look out the window any second."

Poison sighed. He bent his knees and lifted the kneeling wise man on his own. Doreen guided him along the path they had made. She opened the passenger door, and Poison scooted the faceless king into place. "Strap him in." Poison said. "I saw a shovel by the door. I'm going to cover our tracks."

As Doreen wrestled the safety belt over the plaster figure, she looked at his face, or rather his facelessness, for the first time. A shudder went through her. She hoped it wasn't a premonition. Her mother sometimes had those, and it creeped Doreen out.

Poison grabbed the shovel from its place by the door. He turned the shovel over and dragged it topside, up along the place where they had walked. The shovel left an obvious path, but it would be impossible to tell who—or even how many—had been there. Poison returned the shovel and ran back to the van. Doreen had managed to get the door closed, and it looked like the faceless king was sitting and waiting for his ride home. Doreen was standing by the back of the van.

"Come on," she said, motioning wildly.

Poison had the door open, and Doreen folded herself behind the rear seat of the van. Poison looked doubtful. Doreen said, "It's not like you're shoving me in the trunk."

Poison closed the lid gently, then pressed it down with his hip to lock it. He ran around and jumped into the driver's seat. "You okay?"

"I'm fine. Go."

"I was talking to the king," Poison said.

Doreen giggled. "Will you just go? I'm already late."

Poison started the van and pulled away. In his rearview mirror, he took a quick look at the Nativity behind him. The shepherds stood out, even in the dim light. They looked much better and much more realistic than the remaining figures. Poison smiled just a small smile of satisfaction. He allowed himself to think, "I'm going to pull this off."

He pushed away the slip of doubt that followed this first thought, but it seemed to stick and he drove quietly out of town with a mixture of euphoric exhilaration and gut-wrenching worry.

※　※　※

Snake pulled the bookstore van into the spot designated for him by the town as his "business spot." He got out of the van and looked around to see if Deputy Royce was hiding behind a corner, ready to pounce and give him a parking ticket for being three inches over the line. Snake hated that Royce made him paranoid this way. He looked down and tried to see the yellow lines on the street, to make sure he was within the space. He didn't see the yellow lines. He didn't see Deputy Royce. He thought about the boxes for books that were sitting just inside the door. A woman whose husband had died last year had dropped off an extensive collection of science fiction paperbacks. They needed to be sorted and categorized and priced. Some of them were quite old, but in excellent shape. They could be worth something. He asked the woman if she would leave her name and phone number. He would gladly call if he found a rare copy of a Heinlein book or something. She said, "Get what you can for them. I don't want 'em. I'm moving to Florida." She left without taking any money or leaving her name. Snake stood in the doorway looking at the boxes of books through the glass:

hours and hours of work. "I need a cup of coffee," he thought.

Although Snake often made comments about the price of coffee at Hylander's, and although he had a coffee maker in the store, he also knew this was the time of year that Hylander started selling something called a Pumpkin Pie Latte. Snake loved these. He would quietly shell out the four bucks for one, and then pour it into his other cup once he got into the store. He didn't like to go into Hylander's. The first time he went in, he'd made the mistake of asking for "a regular."

The girl behind the counter had asked, "A regular what?"

Snake had ventured, "Coffee?"

She'd asked, "What flavor?"

It was then that Snake knew he was in the wrong place. He made matters worse when he said he wanted "large." The girl, all of seventeen, explained that they did not sell small, medium, or large. They sold petite, standard, and great. That had been the first and last time that Snake had gone into a Hylander Coffee...until last year.

Last year, at about this time of year, a woman had come into the bookshop carrying a Hylander cup. Snake had been immediately enthralled by the aroma. "Excuse me, but what are you drinking?"

"It's a Pumpkin Pie Latte," she said, "Doesn't it smell wonderful?"

It did. Later that morning, he ducked out of the store for five minutes and bought himself one. The taste of a Pumpkin Pie Latte pretty much covered over any embarrassment or wound to his pride.

This morning when he walked in, he was immediately struck by the silence. A girl behind the counter, who looked no more than twelve—save for the nose ring which made her look more like fifteen—said, quietly but professionally, "Good morning, welcome to Hylander Coffee, can I help you?"

Snake looked around the room. The shop was full, but no one was speaking.

He looked at the girl's nametag, which said "Chloe." He said, "I thought you played classical music in the mornings."

She said, "We usually do, but today everyone wants to hear the weasel on the radio."

"The what?"

"The weasel on the radio," she said again. To Snake, it sounded like a Warren Zevon song.

"What's the weasel on the radio?" Snake asked.

Chloe pointed up toward the speaker in the ceiling. Snake followed her finger, and saw that the whole room seemed enraptured by the voice of one man speaking from above.

"It's wrong. It's just plain wrong," said Zack Wright from the speaker installed in the ceiling. "There's something to be said for tradition. There's something to be said for respect for the original intent."

Molly leaned forward, and Snake did too. "His name is Zack Wright, and he thinks he always is right."

Snake was familiar with Zack Wright, but he had never listened to his show for any length of time. The billboards were enough for him to turn the radio off and listen to some Elvis.

"Some people say he's the prophet of truth," Chloe said.

"But you think he's a weasel on the radio," Snake answered. One or two faces had now turned in their direction, as if to say "Shhhhhhhhhh."

"You don't do this all the time?" Snake whispered.

"No," Chloe said. "Usually it's Mozart, but today everyone wants to hear what he's saying about the shepherds."

"The shepherds," Snake repeated. "Is that a local team I don't know about?"

"No," Chloe said, "the shepherds in front of the church. They disappeared a while ago, and now they're back—but the wise men are gone."

Snake looked out the window in the direction of the church. "The shepherds came back?"

Chloe nodded.

"By themselves?" Snake asked. He was trying to kid with her, but she didn't pick up on it.

"Somebody repainted them," she said. Then she looked around from side to side, as if someone might hear her. She leaned in close, and Snake did too. In the softest of whispers (which let Snake know that Chloe was a smoker), she said: "They aren't white anymore."

"What color are they?" Snake asked, still not quite understanding what the problem was. At that moment, he was actually picturing that they had come back painted a royal blue.

"They're sort of brown," Chloe said in her normal voice.

A woman at a nearby table leaned over and said, "Middle Eastern."

Someone at another table shushed her. Zack Wright continued speaking from the ceiling. "Too many denominations are switching to politically correct hymns. There are churches out there who are praying to 'Our Father/Mother in heaven.' There are churches that are trying to take any male references out of the Bible. What I want to know is—where do we draw the line? What is the Summer Park Church doing about this?

"Are they going to paint the statues back to normal? Are they endorsing this? Are the police checking into this? Is this even a crime? Is this some sort of publicity stunt?"

Snake looked around the room. About half the room was nodding, and about half the room was shaking their heads in disgust. However, everyone was listening. Zack Wright said, "Let's go to the phone…. Hello, you're on the Zack Wright Show."

A woman's voice said, "Hi, Zack, I love your show."

Zack Wright replied, "Thank you."

The woman continued, "What I'm most concerned about is…. what sort of message this sends to the children. If the Summer Park Church wants to be politically correct, that doesn't mean the whole community has to be a part of it. Some of us still respect tradition."

"Absolutely," Zack Wright said. "Isn't there anything the liberals can keep their hands off of? Isn't there anything they can't ruin for the rest of us....Emmelton, Pennsylvania...you're on the Zack Wright Show."

This time, it was a man's voice. "Hi, Zack. I love your show."

Zack Wright said: "Thank you."

"What it comes down to is: 'Nobody knows.' Nobody really knows what Jesus' parents looked like. Nobody knows what the shepherds looked like. I'm all for inclusiveness, but I grew up with that image that everybody else did of the stable and the manger and the shepherds. That's what Christmas is. Why do we have to mess with that?"

Snake watched the way the room was listening. He stared at Chloe, who still had the end of her pencil on the pad. She was looking at the speaker in the ceiling as if it might have been a TV there.

Snake said, "Chloe?"

The girl with the nose ring said, "Huh?" and then, "Oh, I'm sorry. What did you want?"

"A Pumpkin Pie Latte, medium...uh, I mean...uh, standard."

Chloe wrote it down, then turned around to make the order, but she was still listening to the radio. From above, Zack Wright said, "The Bible says that they came from the east, right? Well, the east of what? Who knows? The books I had when I was a kid all had pictures of three old white guys on camels. Come on—what's wrong with that? Why do we have to mess with something that has been in place for years?"

Snake stepped out of the building. Rather than turn right toward the bookstore, he turned left and headed toward the church. On the street, he thought about the people inside: all of them transfixed by Zack Wright's voice, all of them listening to what he had to say about the statues. The fact of the matter was that Zack Wright probably had not seen the statues yet. Zack Wright was in Butler, for cryin' out loud, and these people were right down the street from the crime scene.

About a dozen or so people stood just outside of the yellow tape, while Deputy Royce and Sheriff Forbes examined the statues. Snake stared too. Without realizing he was speaking aloud, he said, "Beautiful."

A woman in a blue coat was standing next to Snake. She said, "Shame, isn't it?"

"What is?" Snake asked.

"Someone would go and do a thing like that."

"Like what?" Snake said. "It looks better."

The woman looked at Snake as if he had a third eye. She made an oh-you're-one-of-those face, and stepped back over to resume a conversation with a woman in a matching coat who looked to be her mother. They both turned and looked at Snake. Snake sipped his latte.

Seeing the shepherds side by side with the other pieces made them stand out all the more. He had seen this Nativity set since they had moved to

Summer Park, when Poison had been about five. Each piece pretty much stood in the same place every year. Over the years, they had been re-painted, usually by someone who didn't know what they were doing. One year, they added animals made out of plywood. Someone had made sheep, and had then glued genuine sheep's wool to the boards. The irony that a live sheep was shorn for the purpose of gluing its hair to a faux sheep was lost on just about everyone. When it rained, the plywood-and-wool sheep doubled in size overnight.

Snake stared at the shepherds. It was as though each hair had been painted. Each fold in the shepherds' robe was delineated. If not for the bright yellow crime scene tape, everyone would have come forward and touched the robes—just to be sure they weren't real fabric. But with the shepherds standing next to the rest of the "players" in the Nativity...there was a difference between the shepherds and the rest. It was a difference that was not lost on the two women who had thought "shame." It was a difference that was not lost on Snake, either. The shepherds had found their way home...most definitely darker.

Snake had learned, over his years traveling across the country, that a person's skin didn't matter when you were cold, tired, or needed to share a tent to stay out of the rain. Snake didn't care about race, color, family history, religious preference, or whom you fell in love with. For Snake, it mostly had to do with whether or not you were an idiot. If you couldn't ride with the pack, you needed to get off the road.

The shepherds now looked Middle Eastern. They had swarthy olive complexions. Their new eyes were darker, and had a not-from-around-here look. They didn't belong in this group of white upper-middle-class statuary. Snake wondered if that was how the shepherds had felt at the real birth. Did they stay off to the side as the rich kings came in with the treasure? Did they feel like outsiders? Shepherding was not a highly respected profession. These two shepherds—who looked similar enough to be brothers and yet different enough to deserve names—looked as if they just might be ready to run if the innkeeper came out and yelled at them.

Snake was so caught up in this daydream that he didn't see Deputy Royce approach him until it was too late.

"Mr. Davenport," Royce said.

He could feel the officer's eyes on him, but he didn't look at him. Snake said, "Deputy."

"Who's minding the store?"

"I'm opening late," Snake said. "Thought I'd come over and see what folks were talking about."

"Hell of a thing," the deputy said. He ran it all together as if it were one word.

Snake said nothing. He didn't know for sure what the deputy thought about the shepherds, but he had a pretty good idea. When Deputy Royce was concerned it was best to keep your mouth shut. Sheriff Forbes looked over to where the Snake and Deputy Royce were standing. He said, "Deputy."

Deputy Royce started to walk away, but he

didn't take his eye away from Snake. Snake tried not to look at the officer, but he could feel the hatred come off of him. He knew the look he was getting. It said, "Don't even think about it. I'm watching you."

The woman in the blue coat took a step further away from Snake. Snake sipped his latte, turned around, and went back to his store.

Chapter 10

On the first day of December the angel Bez-A-Lel visited Poison in the family garage, Deputy Danny Royce visited his mother in the nursing home, and a woman named Nicole visited her boss in the offices of Pittsburgh television station KADK with an idea.

Poison stood looking face to face with the tallest of the three wise men. For some reason, Poison had decided that this meant that this particular wise man was also the eldest, perhaps the wisest, of the wise men. Poison took great care in painting the lines in the king's face. Poison had looked up various accounts of the wise men in some books he had found in his father's store. He had wound up going back to the Scriptures and finding only that they "came from the east." Poison decided they were probably not what so many of the books depict: a trio consisting of a black man, a white man, and an Asian. He also found no references in the Bible to the wise men's names. So he was on his own.

The eldest king's robe had been completed for a few days now. In fact, all the kings were nearly done. Poison had worked on all three of them at once and was impressed at how well he was doing. The faceless king, who now shared a cloned face with one of the shepherds, was the most difficult. Poison had attached the new face with a fiberglass patch, then spent hours lightly sanding the edges down. The first coat of primer had all but covered any ridges in the kneeling king's skin. Poison decided that this king was the youngest, and that the other two were allowing their young colleague to present his gift first. The kneeling king held a box, which very well could have been a box of gold. The wisest king held what Poison thought was a bottle. So this, Poison figured, was frankincense. The last king held a jar: myrrh. Poison didn't know what sort of containers myrrh and frankincense were carried in, but these made sense to him. He made a mental note to have the oldest wise man look, not at the baby, but at the kneeling king placing his gift before the manger.

Each king's robe was a different color, but the capes that covered their shoulders were similar in length and style, so Poison assumed they should be the same. Perhaps this cape was a way of showing the world your place.

"As if the crown weren't a giveaway," Poison said to the eldest. He got no response, of course—but, with all that he had gone through so far, hearing an answer would not have surprised him all that much.

Poison had painted each king's robe a deep purple. He had perfected an unusual stroke that gave the purple paint a smooth look. Then, he'd taken the brush his father had used to paint the house a few years ago and dabbed it across the wet purple paint. The result looked as if it had texture, like velvet.

"In case you find yourself needing to pay a visit," Poison said to the old king. "The only king we have that wears velvet is Elvis, and he's been dead almost as long as you have."

He had started talking to the figures soon after they had arrived in his garage. Part of this was because he needed someone to talk to when Doreen wasn't there. Part of this was because he hadn't been getting a lot of sleep and didn't care how silly he looked. Mostly, though, he talked to them because he felt down deep inside that if he treated them as if they were alive it would affect the paint job.

He had found an old bar stool in the corner of the garage and had been sitting on it as he worked on the two standing kings. He was putting the finishing touches on the crown of the oldest King. It was a simple crown—there were no jewels and very little carving. Poison took this to mean that the oldest king didn't need to show off. His kingly nature would show through his eyes and his body language, not through his ornaments.

The youngest king's crown was covered in jewels. Poison had painted their colors in the order they appeared in the rainbow. There were exactly enough "jewels" to go through the color list four times. Poison remembered when Doreen's mother had taught them about color in art class. She had introduced them to Mr. Roy G. Biv—a name that listed the colors of the rainbow in order: Red, Orange, Yellow, Green, Blue, Indigo, and Violet. Poison had started calling the youngest king Roy.

Doreen had not been by the garage in a few days. He told her he was going to start taking pictures of the kings, but she quietly pointed out to her befuddled insomniac boyfriend that taking pictures of the evidence only served to help the prosecution, should the prosecution need any help.

"She's smarter than I am," Poison told the old king. "A lot smarter. How about you? You married? You got a wise woman at home?"

A voice behind him said, "Most of them had more than one wife."

"You know," Poison said. "I always wondered if God listened in when we were being idiots—and, if he did, why he didn't spend more time laughing."

Bez-A-Lel the angel said, "God is everywhere. He is above all things and in all things and through all things."

"So he does listen to us," Poison said without turning around.

"Yes," the angel said.

"Does he giggle?"

"Sometimes," Bez-A-Lel said, "but in the way that a parent laughs at a child who's making all those baby-noises in a crib or singing to itself in the car seat."

The angel was close behind him now. He had examined Roy and was now looking closely at the second wise man. "You do good work."

"Thank you," Poison said. "Am I to assume that my choice of ideas with which to 'use my gifts' is acceptable in the eyes of God?"

"You should never assume anything when it comes to God," Bez-A-Lel said.

"I suppose not. How do you know when God is happy?"

"He laughs."

"Have you heard it?"

"God's laugh?"

"Yes. Is it one of those smirk laughs, or is it one of those big guffaws that make everybody else around laugh too?"

Bez-A-Lel stopped and floated for a moment. "It's like nothing you've ever heard."

"Oh, c'mon, give me something," Poison begged. Using a larger brush, he dabbed a brass-gold paint across the front of the king's crown.

Bez-A-Lel thought for a moment, then asked, "Have you ever watched one of those blooper shows where people mess up their lines and try to act like they know what they're doing—but they start shaking and then suddenly burst out laughing so hard they fall down?"

Poison dragged a dry brush over the area of the crown he had just painted. It blended a dark brown with a muted gold, giving the crown a look of patina. He nodded.

"It's a lot like that."

"So he's laughing at us."

"He's laughing," the angel confirmed..

Poison continued to work. Eventually he said, "Are you just here to play art critic, or is there some specific reason?"

"I'm not a critic."

"Sorry. I'm cranky. No sleep, ya know?"

"Angels don't sleep unless we want to. Like eating—we do it only for the pleasure."

"What do angels dream about?" Poison asked.

"Mostly about humans."

"So why are you here?"

"You have a concern. You're worried about something."

"I'm worried about getting caught."

"That's not it. You've got something else going on in your head."

"I'm worried about Doreen. Do you remember when I asked about others getting hurt, and you said it was a possibility?"

The angel was now bending low to look up into the face of Roy the kneeler. "I remember."

"Could I get a little more information on that one? I don't want her to get in trouble. I don't want her to get hurt."

"You brought her into this."

"Maybe I shouldn't have."

"Maybe."

"You're not going to give me anything on this, are you?"

"God is pleased with you," the angel said.

Poison looked at the king and asked, "Do you ever feel like you're talking to a brick wall?"

After hearing no more words and sensing that he was once again alone, Poison turned around and saw that he was right. To the king he said, "I thought he'd never leave."

He began to wonder if telling Doreen was a good idea after all.

❆ ❆ ❆

Danny Royce pulled into the Eden's Rest Assisted Living Facility. He was still in uniform. His mother had told him once that she was proud of what he did for a living, so he wore his uniform whenever he came to visit her. She hadn't usually used words like "proud" when he was growing up.

He used the comb in his glove compartment to straighten his short hair. He picked up the bouquet of flowers he'd bought at the grocery store and went inside.

Most of the nurses and therapists who worked at Eden's Rest knew him by now. Most waved a polite hello and continued with what they were doing. Danny Royce had made an effort to let them know that he was a cop and that he was not going to put up with anything less than perfect service for his mother.

Eleanor Royce smiled when her son came into the game room. The room had a number of tables where the residents could play checkers and cards. Danny's mother was a whiz at poker, when she could remember what beats what. She had a poker face that no one could see through.

He said "Hi, Mom," and kissed her cheek. She reached up and patted his. Most people would have easily guessed Danny to be her grandson.

Eleanor had had Danny in her late forties. His father, before he left, had thrown around the words "mistake" and "accident" when he'd been drinking. His mother had had a stroke on his birthday when she was seventy. He couldn't keep her at home, and he was constantly applying for every type of financial aid he could get to keep his mother in the nicest place he could.

"This is my son," Eleanor said to a woman across the table. The woman was nearly a hundred but she seemed more coherent than his mother most of the time. "My son is a sheriff."

"Deputy," Danny corrected, "but someday, who knows?"

It was a conversation that they had every time he visited. The people at his mother's card table knew it by heart and didn't care one way or another about Eleanor Royce's boy's career ambitions. They wanted to know when supper was.

"I fold," Eleanor said, tossing her cards into the center of the table. "What are you going to do with three sixes anyway? C'mon, Danny, take me back to my room and we can put those in a vase."

As he turned his mother away from the table, a man named Kent—who was eighty, and was considered quite a catch by some of the women in the home—peeked at Eleanor's cards and said, "She was bluffing. I knew it."

In her room, Danny Royce pushed his mother's chair up to a table where she had been working on a jigsaw puzzle of a nude man. "Mother, where did you get this?"

"Elmira Blake," Eleanor said, "but the nurse confiscated all the best parts. I'm trying to keep my eyes sharp."

"Where's the vase I bought you?" Danny asked, pinching the bridge of his nose.

"In the bathroom cupboard beneath the sink."

Danny walked in and took a quick inventory of the room. There were a few more pill bottles than last month. Last month he had noticed blood on her toothbrush. This time it was a new toothbrush.

"Stop inspecting my bathroom, Danny," his mother called from the outer apartment.

Danny emerged a moment later with a vase. "So how are you, Mom?"

"What's going on with the statues, Danny?"

"The what?"

"I was listening to that man on the radio and ..."

"Mom, I told you not to listen to him. He just gets you all worked up."

"I'm not worked up." Eleanor Royce pushed herself back from the table and rolled to the bureau, where she pulled a pair of scissors out of the drawer. She began snipping the ends off the stems of the flowers that her son had brought her. She snipped with such intensity that Danny wondered what she was picturing in her mind when she made each cut.

"A bunch of kids probably took the statues," Danny said. "We'll find 'em."

"They said some of them came back already." SNIP

"The shepherds were replaced."

"They said they were painted to look like they were terrorists." SNIP

"Not terrorists, Mom. They're shepherds. Shepherds are not terrorists."

"I don't know why you don't do something about it." SNIP

"We're kind of short-handed, Mom. You know that?"

"Well, you could set up a surveillance or something." SNIP

"Mom, I'm going to do that."

"Catch them. Put them in jail. Show them we don't put up with that in America." SNIP

"Mom, this is Summer Park, Pennsylvania. There are no terrorists."

"This is how they start." Eleanor pointed at him with the scissors. "This is how they start, and pretty soon they'll be running this country, and our sorry-assed police force is just going to stand by and watch it happen." SNIP.

The last stem lost the last inch of its bottom, and Eleanor started with the first one again. SNIP. Danny took the flowers and put them in the vase and arranged them as his mother continued to talk about terrorists. He carefully took the scissors from her and put them back in the drawer.

"Your father, now, there was a man. He didn't put up with crap from anybody. He'd take those terrorist kids and bash their heads together."

Danny thought, "My father used to throw you down the stairs." But he didn't say anything. He felt like he was getting smaller inside his uniform as he sat and listened to his mother continue. Eventually she would run out of steam and he would lay her in her bed and then he would go.

Nicole Hamilton was still in love with her job. The hours were lousy and the pay was worse but she had a stack of business cards on her at all times that said "KADK-TV" in bright red letters. Beneath the station logo was her name, and beneath her name were the words "Production" and "Research." It was the four letters "KADK" that made the job worthwhile. When she was in kindergarten and came home from school at lunchtime, she didn't turn on cartoons or put in sing-along videos. Nicole watched the KADK Noontime News with Dan Harding. She used to imitate the announcer's deep voice and say, "And now...here's Dan Harding."

When Dan Harding said, "Good afternoon, Pittsburgh," Nicole would say, "Good afternoon, Dan Harding."

She loved the TV station the way some of her friends loved boy-bands. Now, here she was, in her own office. Okay, right now it was a desk she shared in the video store room (a/k/a The Trench). The guy she shared a desk with was Kyle, who was nice enough but never had any ambition of getting out of The Trench. Nicole wanted to be out there, on the scene. Not on camera but producing the news: pointing for the cameraman to focus his lens on the burning building, being there when the rescue workers pulled the 98-year-old grandmother from her roof just before her home was washed away.

She wanted to produce. She had gone along as an assistant on two assignments. One had been for election results; the other had been for a teachers' strike. Neither assignment really required an assistant producer, but she had made herself so much "in the way" that Richard, the senior segment producer, had sent her along to get her out of his office.

KADK had signed a deal, and was now one of the few cable stations that could be seen nationwide: around the world, for those with satellite technology.

Nicole's job was to peruse newspapers from around the country. She spent every day looking for cute human-interest stories and passing them on to the copywriters who might, or might not, choose to use them on the air. KADK had recently started using one of those low screen-crawl graphics that kept the viewers up to date on the weather and the latest Hollywood gossip.

Nicole believed in Jimmy Buffett's advice that, if you did your job to the absolute best of your ability (no matter how bad it was), that was the quickest way to a job that sucks less. It was dark outside, but the KADK building still hummed—with Nicole alone... She preferred to work late because she felt she got more done when Kyle went home. She also felt that, when people walked by her office and saw her reading the newspaper, they questioned her ability or just thought she was lazy. She sipped her Hylander Coffee (which was now cold) and studied the Summer Park Times, looking for any interesting bits that might get passed along to the upper levels of research. She had been an employee of KADK for six months. So far, two bits she had uncovered had made it to the news crawl at the bottom of the screen. She had called her mother in Texas, who had videotaped the crawl.

A man in a white shirt, his tie undone, walked past her door. His name was Richard. He had his own office: smaller than the one Nicole shared, but he had it all to himself. "It's okay to go home," he said.

She looked up and smiled. "I know. I'm almost done."

"Anything interesting?"

She looked down again. "Here's a town in Pennsylvania that had a life-sized Nativity statue stolen and then replaced with restored politically correct copies."

"You're kidding," Richard said. He set his brief-case on the floor and leaned against the door jamb. "What does it mean by 'politically correct'?"

Nicole looked down again. She brushed her hair out of her face and tucked it behind her ear. It was a move that Richard found very adorable. Nicole wasn't aware she had done it. "It says that the shepherd statues vanished one night and then reappeared with a new paint job, and now they actually look like they are from the Middle East."

"You mean not like white people?"

"Yep," Nicole said. "Now the wise men have disappeared and the whole town is waiting to see if they show up again and if they get a paint job too."

"Hnnn," Richard said. He bent over, picked up his briefcase, and said, "If they show up and Jesus goes missing, let me know. Might be worth a mention. Good night."

"'Night," she said. She waited until she heard his footsteps disappear down the hall, then checked her watch. She wondered how quickly she could get her hands on tomorrow's—well, now it would be today's—Summer Park Times.

❄ ❄ ❄

Jack Lambert was a big kid. In fact, Jack had never been called a "little kid" even when he had been one. He had always been "big for his age" or "my, he's a big boy, isn't he?"

Jack played football, basketball, and baseball for Summer Park High School. He kept his grades just high enough to stay on the teams—though there were times when he needed a little "extra help" and the coaches were more than willing to quietly look the other way. Jack kept his 2.2 average and just about everybody seemed happy—except those who were smaller than Jack (which meant just about everybody else in the student body).

Jack liked to bump people into lockers and smack their books out of their hands as the halls filled with people between classes. Underclassmen learned, in the first few days of school, to avoid Jack. Most students would yell, or say something, but usually you just picked up your stuff and moved on with your life. Jack didn't pick on other athletes, girls, or kids who looked like they had spent time in juvenile hall. Fortunately for Jack, this left a wide variety of victims.

Poison had lost his books to Jack Lambert's "jokes" more than once. He knew better than to get into a fight with Jack. He'd once shouted a few clever insults to Jack's back, that everyone around had laughed at, but that Jack didn't get. Even when his friends had explained it to him, he still didn't get the joke.

Mostly, Jack left Poison alone. It was easier to pick on someone that didn't make him feel stupid.

Poison hadn't slept in two days. Trying to get the work done on the wise men was killing him. They were a lot more detailed than the shepherds were. They had more robes, and each king carried a box that was covered in jewels or some sort of treasure. The faceless wise man, the one who was kneeling, was currently kneeling on the workbench in the garage.

This morning, Poison had checked the fiberglass patch that was fastening the king's new face: it seemed to be holding well. He could start painting tonight.

He was tired and grouchy. The test he should have studied for was over; he was hoping he had at least passed. Somehow he'd thought that, since he was doing this mission for God, the angel would slip him some answers—but that didn't happen.

Poison was starting to get resentful. He wondered if Moses had ever started to feel this way. Moses had had to wander around for forty years. He must have gotten sick and tired of it at some point. Poison had checked his Bible, though, and there were very few accounts of the great Bible heroes saying, "That's it, God, I'm done."

Poison had read Job's rant—but God's reply had gone on for pages, and had essentially said, "Are you God? No? Then shut up."

Poison had been thinking of these things, and of Doreen, and of his parents' real Christmas gift—which he had not made, but would have to—and of an upcoming quiz in biology or math, he couldn't remember which. He suddenly felt a familiar shove at his back and a slap at the books in his hand, spreading his books and papers out over the floor to be immediately lost in the web of student feet. He immediately knew the cause, even before he looked up and saw Jack Lambert looking back over his shoulder. Jack turned to his friends, laughed, and said, "What a loser."

Poison looked down and saw he still had one book in his hand. It was the latest book by Christopher Moore. Poison had read all of Christopher Moore's books. Next to Mark Twain, Moore was Poison's favorite author. He had been trying to finish this book for a week, but hadn't found the time.

It seemed like a waste of a book to do what he was about to do. He doubted he was going to get it back. Later, when Poison thought about what he had done, it played back in his brain in slow motion—but while it was happening, just his arm was in slow motion. The rest of him probably could have stopped the throw, but his other hand was cement. Christopher Moore's latest novel left Poison's hand, sailing through the air in a nice, clean pitch that bounced solidly off Jack Lambert's head.

Poison remembered, later, how red Jack's face had been when he charged. He didn't really remember much after that, except the hand of Ms. Szuch on the back of his collar as she yanked the two of them apart.

❄   ❄   ❄

Deputy Danny Royce sat at his desk with a sheet of paper in his hand. He was trying to convince himself that he was working, but he hadn't read a word. In fact, if anyone had been paying attention they would have noticed that the paper in his hand was shaking too much to be read at all. Deputy Royce was listening to the radio in the other room. Rhonda, their part-time receptionist, listened to Zack Wright every day.

Zack Wright was saying "...across the street from the police station. I mean right across the street. You can stand in the middle of the church lawn and look at the front door of the police station."

Deputy Royce's scowl deepened, and the crease in his forehead suddenly made him look much older.

"Which means that, not once but twice, someone walked onto the front lawn of the church and walked away with life-sized statues, and Summer Park's finest never saw a thing. Could someone call up and tell me—right now—have you ever seen any member of Summer Park's police force actually solve a crime? I know most of you have gotten traffic tickets, but I'm talking about a real honest-to-goodness criminal act. Has anyone ever seen the Summer Park Police Department in action? Let's go to the phone. Hi, you're on the Zack Wright Show."

A woman's voice said, "The Summer Park Police Department is drastically under-funded and under-manned. Every time they try to increase their budget, the city council votes it down. How can you operate a police department with two officers and a part-time receptionist?"

Danny Royce bowed his head. He felt a low pain begin deep in his brain. He whispered. "Oh, God, no. No, mother. No."

Danny heard the outer office door open and Sheriff Forbes' voice say, "Rhonda, I asked you not to listen to that in the office. You want music, fine—but turn off that crap."

The tone of his voice let Danny know that his

boss had been listening in the car, or had stopped for a coffee and been razzed by the folks in the coffee shop. He cleared his throat and looked down at the paper in his hand. He saw it was shaking, so he set it down flat on the desk and pretended to be reading. He heard the radio tuner fuzz, and then heard Perry Como's voice singing "The First Noel."

Sheriff Forbes came into the three-desk room and sat down hard on his chair. The third desk had been put in place in anticipation of hiring a third officer, but at the last minute the city council had turned down the funding request. Forbes looked over at his deputy, who had not looked up. "This is going to get worse before it gets better, isn't it?"

Deputy Royce wondered what his mother was saying to the ears of Summer Park, and whether Zack Wright had gotten her to admit that she was the mother of one of Summer Park's finest. He wondered if she would start talking about him playing cops-and-robbers as a kid. He wondered if she would start threatening to egg Zack Wright's car, as she had threatened when Wright had decided to rant about teachers getting an increase in salary.

Deputy Royce's mother was a retired schoolteacher. The family had moved to Summer Park while Danny was still in the police academy. Three days after they moved in, Danny's father had had a massive stroke and died. Danny had gotten a job in the local police force, and his mother had started substitute teaching. Three years now, and none of the students had figured out that the crazy old lady who came in when the Language Arts teacher was sick was the mother of the cop who would run them in if they were out past curfew. She had been a teacher in his high school, which had made his life unbearable. He had been picked on mercilessly. When he became a cop the teasing had stopped. He liked being a cop. He liked carrying a gun. He didn't have much opportunity to use it, or even to draw it out of the holster, for that matter. He still practiced twice a week. He was a marksman. Now, as he sat in the little shared office, he tried to bury the little part of him that hoped that—when they caught the person who was taking the Nativity statues—the culprit might just for a moment run or resist arrest. He pushed this feeling down deep, along with the hope that someday Zack Wright would be pulled over for speeding. There were a lot of other feelings held down there.

What Deputy Danny Royce didn't understand was that hiding these thoughts below the surface was like holding a beach ball under the water. Eventually you either let go, or it got away from you.

Chapter 11

Sheriff Forbes always drove one loop around the town before going to the office. Since his wife had passed away, he had found that routine helped him not think about the fact that he was alone. His alarm clock was set for the same time every morning. He would shower, shave, shampoo, and be dried off at exactly the same time. He could put two eggs into a pan and two slices of bread in the toaster, and each morning they would be done the same moment. The toast would pop. He would slide the egg between the slices and he would read the paper until his sandwich was gone. The coffee was always done in time for him to pour himself a travel mug full, and be out the door, every morning by seven-thirty. In the last few years, he had never left before 7:29 and never after 7:34. He did it all without thinking. The drive to work took 17 minutes. He would arrive about an hour before Danny Royce, and the two of them would discuss what the day would entail—which was rarely different than what had happened the day before.

He drove through town, giving everything a quick once over. He could spot things that were different. He knew who opened their stores early and who opened late. Many would be open early today for sales. He knew the Hylander Coffee Shop opened at 7:45. There were weeks when he could drive past the shop right at the moment the lights came on.

This morning, driving up Fulton Street, he spotted the squad car. He slowed to a stop. The squad car was supposed to be in back of the station. He got out of the car and walked toward the driver's side door. The windows were steamed, and when he opened the door, his deputy fell out onto the pavement.

"Ohhhhhhhhhhhhhhhhhhhh," Danny said. "My God, it's cold." He was on his feet and hugging himself and jumping up and down in place.

"Danny, have you been there all night?"

"What ddddo you mean all nnu-nu-nu-night? What tt-t-ime is it?"

"Almost eight in the morning."

Danny stopped jumping, but his chin was shivering. He had never been so cold in his life. Sheriff Forbes said, "You're lucky you didn't freeze to death."

"I was ssssss-sssstaking out the cc-c-c-chh-chchh-church. I wa wanted t-t-t-to…" but his voice stopped cold and he looked past Sheriff Forbes' shoulder. Quietly he said "N-n-n-n-nn-no NO." He started to run, but his joints had stiffened and he fell again. "Ahhhh!"

Sheriff Forbes helped the deputy to his feet and watched him take off. Danny Royce's freezing cold body was suddenly alive with red-hot anger. The sheriff looked toward the church, and saw what Danny saw. "Oh, God," he said and knew that his routine would not be routine at all.

❉   ❉   ❉

Reverend Tumbler was wearing his Taft State hockey jersey. He was totally baffled by it. He'd never played a game of hockey in his life. He'd never watched the game. He'd never even skated. He had never told anyone about a secret desire to play hockey…probably because he didn't have one. He had never even used the phrase "H-E-double-hockey-sticks." He hadn't gone to Taft State, and—as far as he knew—the only thing he liked about hockey was a song by Warren Zevon about a hockey player named Buddy.

His wife had bought the shirt for him about a month before the accident. When the credit card bill came in, he saw a fifty-dollar charge to the Sport Shack. He spent an entire Saturday searching through the house, trying to find the spot where his wife liked to hide his Christmas gifts. In the guest bathroom behind the towels, he found a box. The jersey was huge. She had paid to have the name TUMBLER written in large block letters across the back. He had no clue why she bought it for him. He wore it as a nightshirt with a pair of sweats, pretty much 365 days a year. He was wearing the shirt on Friday morning when his bell rang at 8:30.

He opened the door to see Harry Vaughn on his stoop. "The wise men are back," Harry said. "Didn't I tell you? Get dressed. I'll meet you at the church."

"And a wonderful morning to you," Tumbler replied.

"Did you hear what I said?"

"Yes, Harry, I heard what you said." Tumbler was still squinting from the light and rubbing the sleep out of his eyes. He wanted coffee.

"Then we have to hurry," Harry said. He was practically vibrating.

"Harry, have you had a lot of coffee already this morning?"

"Never touch it," Harry said. "It makes you impotent."

Reverend Tumbler considered this for a second. He had never heard of this particular side effect from coffee, but if Harry said it, then Harry believed it. He was going to ask where Harry had gotten this particular piece of information, when a cold breeze came in from the open door and across his bare toes.

"Let me ask you something, Harry..." He motioned Harry to come closer. Harry leaned in, and Tumbler said, "Do you think they're going anywhere in the next hour?" When he got no response other than a dirty look, Tumbler said, "Harry, I'll be there in an hour or so."

Harry Vaughn turned on his heel and headed back toward his car. Tumbler called out, "Harry?"

Harry turned.

"How do they look?"

Harry said, "Remember we had one black, one white, and one yellow?"

"Asian," Tumbler corrected.

Harry rolled his eyes, "Asian then. Remember?"

"Yeah." Tumbler said.

"Well," Harry said, "now they're all the same color." He got in his car and drove off.

"Hmmm," the minister pondered. "I wonder what color." He was still standing in the doorway of his house when Jenny the papergirl walked by and handed him the paper. "You play hockey in college, Reverend?"

"Until they kicked me off the team for excessive violent behavior."

"Cool," the girl said, and moved on. Tumbler closed the door and went to the kitchen to make a pot of coffee.

❄ ❄ ❄

About the same time as Sheriff Forbes was leaving his house, and a half hour before he opened the squad car door that would dump his deputy to the pavement, Poison and his Dad were in the kitchen. His father was shoving various leftovers into their green camping cooler. They were on their way to the bookstore. The annual "Book 'Em, Danno" After-Thanksgiving Pre-Christmas Sale would start at 9:00. They were going in early, so that Poison could make a sign to hang outside. Snake was bouncing back and forth between the refrigerator and the kitchen table. He was actually whistling.

Poison leaned against the sink. He was eating a Pop-Tart. Poison and Brenda (who shared a hatred of mornings) watched Snake bounce back and forth as if they were watching a tennis match. Brenda was holding her coffee mug in her hand. She had been dunking one of the ginger cookies that Iza had sent home with them, but she had dozed off for a few seconds and lost part of the cookie in her cup. She was trying to fish it out with her spoon. "You want coffee?" she asked.

"Nope," Snake said. "It's going to be a good day. I'm going to treat my son to a latte."

Poison looked at his mother. She looked back and shrugged her shoulders. "You're treating your son to a what?" Poison asked.

"I'm treating you to a latte," Snake said. "I had one from that coffee shop down the street from the store the other day." The Tupperware square made a snap as it closed around a second piece of pumpkin pie.

"Okay," Poison said. He knew there was a joke buried deep in there someplace, but he was too tired to go digging for it.

Snake disappeared through the kitchen door toward the living room. "Five minutes," he shouted, as if he were announcing a bus departure. "Five minutes."

Brenda lifted the last part of the ginger cookie

out of her coffee and ate it off the spoon. "Did you get Doreen home okay?"

Poison nodded.

"I like Iza a lot," Brenda said. "Ted's a little stiff, but Iza is a trip. How did those two wind up together?"

"Long story. Have Doreen tell you. She tells it better than I could. Apparently it involves poetry and an island vacation."

"What did she seem so mad about?" Brenda asked.

"When?" Poison asked.

"Last night, before you took her home."

"You were watching us?" Poison asked. At that moment, he was genuinely more concerned that she knew what was in the garage than he was that his mother had been eavesdropping.

"'S'go," Snake said as he breezed through the kitchen. He bent to kiss Brenda on the cheek and went out the door. "'S'go" apparently meant "Let us make haste, my son, and be gone to my place of business."

Poison put the rest of the Pop-Tart in his mouth and followed his dad out the door, glad to be away from the conversation with his mother.

"I'll be in at noon," Brenda called after they had left the room. The side door closed ,and she added "-ish." She reached into the Ziploc bag on the table and grabbed another one of Iza Hudson's ginger cookies.

❄   ❄   ❄

Inside Hylander Coffee, Molly the waitress was trying as hard as she could to simply get the coffee and not listen to the radio—but she was getting worried. The room seemed to be slowly dividing itself into two distinct factions: those who simply repeated the "Wright is Right" mantra, and those who thought it was about time that a little change happened in a little town that hadn't had any change in a long time. Each time a point was made, either by a caller or by the host, half the room would murmur its agreement. Each time, it got a little louder.

Snake and Poison walked in. Snake went right to the counter. Poison hung back, hoping he might see Doreen or hoping that Molly wouldn't recognize him and make some comment like "Where's your girlfriend?"

Snake looked at the ceiling and winced as Zack Wright's voice babbled about political correctness. "Two Pumpkin Pie Lattes to go," he said. He looked around and asked, "People come by before they hit the after-Thanksgiving sales?" There was a hint of hope in his voice.

"You don't want to be in here anyway," Molly said. She didn't say it very loud.

"It does seem a little tense. What's going on?"

"You drove by what's going on." She nodded out the door. Snake turned, looking past his son, to the growing crowd over near the churchyard.

"Oh, no, not again," he said.

"Yep," Molly said. "The wise men came back."

"All by themselves?" Snake asked, but Molly wasn't in a joking mood.

"Dad, let's go," Poison said quietly from the door. He didn't want to look behind him.

"Getting nasty in here," Molly said, as she added the steamed milk to the first paper cup. "Nobody tips when it's nasty."

"Dad," Poison said again, a little more impatient this time.

Someone nearby said, "Shhhh."

Molly looked at Poison. "You look like you were up late."

"Letterman was throwing stuff off the roof again," Poison said. He had no idea if it was true.

"I love it when they do that. What'd they throw?"

Someone nearby said "Shhh."

Snake looked out the window and asked, "How do they look?"

"The wise men?" Molly asked.

Snake nodded.

"Brown," she said. Poison still hadn't turned to look out the window. Snake turned to his son and said, "Let's go take a look."

Poison said, "No, Dad, let's go open the store."

"I'll just be a minute," Snake said.

"If you're going over...." Molly said—then leaned and made a "come here" motion with her head. Snake came closer. "The sheriff is already over there. Tell him to stop by here. It's really getting tense."

Snake half-smiled. Molly leaned over the counter, confiding. "I'm serious. It's mean in here. I know when people are just itching for something to happen. If you guys are really wandering over to the church and you see the good Reverend, send him over. This place is going to get nasty. We need a peacemaker. Just tell somebody we're sitting on a grenade, okay?"

The father and son took their cups and wandered out of the store. Snake shoved a few dollars into the tip jar by the register. "Let's go over to the church."

By the time the two of them reached the yellow police tape, there was already a crowd. Many were holding small pocket radios. One man had a boom box. He was listening to Zack Wright. The people with earphones in their ears were nodding—Poison decided they were listening to the same show. Poison was looking everywhere except at the statues.

Out of the corner of his eye, he saw Deputy Royce. Poison wondered how long he had slept in the car. From the look of him, Poison guessed it was most of the night. The only thing that overshadowed his exhaustion was the fact that the good deputy looked really, really angry. Deputy Royce was talking to the sheriff, or rather he was nodding to the sheriff as the sheriff spoke in tones only his deputy could hear. Poison didn't know what was being said, but he judged from the deputy's face that it was a compliment.

"Wow," Snake said.

"Wow, what?" Poison asked.

"The statues. They're amazing."

Poison turned and looked at the statues for the first time in the daylight. He thought, "Yeah, I know," but he didn't say it out loud.

Deputy Royce strolled quietly over to where Snake and Poison were standing. Poison whispered under his breath, "Houston, we have a problem."

Snake looked up and said something under his breath that Poison had never heard his father say.

Deputy Royce said, "Morning, gentlemen."

"Deputy," Snake said. Royce turned toward Poison, who was looking elsewhere on purpose. Snake nudged him.

"Morning," Poison said.

"What brings you two here on this cold day?"

Snake and Poison looked at each other. Poison said, "You're serious, right?"

Deputy Royce shot him a look that made him look away again. Snake said, "We went for coffee, and someone told us about the statues. Thought we'd come take a look."

❄ ❄ ❄

Bill Tumbler parked in the back of the church, rather than in his assigned "Pastor" parking space. He pulled the Cleveland Browns stocking cap down over his ears as he got out of his car. It would occur to him later that he probably already had done enough to alienate people in a town this close to

Pittsburgh, and that some other hat would have been more appropriate.

Harry Vaughn caught him as he came around the corner of the front yard. Harry looked at the cap and shook his head. "Reverend, we've got a crowd."

Bill Tumbler said, "So I see."

"I've already called the Gazette and I..."

"You called the paper?" Tumbler asked.

"Yeah," Harry Vaughn said. There was just a hint of "Well, duh" in his voice.

"Why did you call the Gazette?"

"We're going to get these guys, Reverend. We're going to get them. Somebody knows something somewhere. Besides, maybe this will bring people in on Christmas Eve for a change."

Rev. Tumbler said nothing. He knew they filled the sanctuary on Christmas Eve and so did Harry, but Harry was in one of his "best interests of the church at heart" moods, and Tumbler knew it was usually a good idea to just let Harry go.

"I wish you had told me first," Tumbler said.

Harry said, "I called the Pittsburgh Press, and guess what? They already knew."

"How did they find out?" Bill Tumbler asked.

"I don't know," Harry said, "They're sending a photographer. They'll probably want to ask you some questions."

"I'm not talking to reporters, Harry."

"I already told them you'd have a statement."

"I don't have a statement."

"I wrote one," Harry said, "but it'd be better coming from you."

Tumbler asked, "Do I really hear Zack Wright talking about our church?"

"Yeah," Harry Vaughn said. (He said it like a small child who was waiting to sit on Santa's lap at the mall.) "Pretty nifty, huh?"

Reverend Tumbler didn't think it was pretty nifty at all.

He turned and looked at the wise men who had found their way back to the front yard of the church.

"Whoever did it did a nice job," he said.

Harry Vaughn said, "Look at them closely, Reverend."

Bill Tumbler looked at them, and then back at Harry, as if to say, "Okay, I have looked at them, and I have seen them. Now what?"

Harry asked, "Don't they look just a little wrong to you?"

"They look better."

"Reverend, they look like taxi drivers."

Bill Tumbler looked into Harry Vaughn's eyes. Every fiber of his being said that 'taxi drivers' was not the phrase Harry wanted to say but it was the one that came out after the first one had been censored by Harry's bigoted little brain.

❊　❊　❊

Inside Hylander's, Molly was hustling back and forth. People were grumpy. Some were standing and looking out the window in the direction of the church. A crew of middle-aged men sat with their backs to the window, to make it seem as if they were just there for the coffee and weren't interested in what was going on behind them at all.

From the speaker: "WKHJ—this is the Zack Wright Show. You're on the air, hello."

"Hello, Zack. It's an honor."

"Thank you," said Wright.

"I wanted to know if you'd heard anything about this rumor going around that there was a police officer on duty last night who was apparently sleeping instead of watching the scene of the crime."

"I had heard that," Zack said. "However, we don't deal in rumors and so far Summer Park's finest has not returned any calls from this station. But it would not surprise me if such a thing was true." There was a click, and Zack Wright said "WKHJ—hello, you're on the Zack Wright Show."

A woman's voice said, "Zack, I'm sitting here with my Bible open and it clearly says 'wise men.' And it had this little index in the back that says 'Magi,' which, according to the book, means 'astrologers.' That's why they followed the star and not a map."

"Men never ask directions anyway," Zack Wright chuckled. "Tell me what your name is, dear."

"Irene," said the woman.

"And you've got your Bible right there?"

"Yes."

"Do me a favor, Irene, and look up Psalm 72." There was a brief pause while Zack Wright quietly whistled "We Three Kings." "Find it yet, love?"

"Yes."

"Read it to me, sweetheart."

Everyone in the shop got a little quieter. Some physically pointed their ears at the speaker as Irene started to read. She read the first nine verses, and then said "The kings of Tarshish and the isles shall bring presents; the kings of Sheba and Seba shall offer gifts. Yea, all kings shall fall down before him. All nations shall serve him."

"There you go," Zack Wright said triumphantly. "If this is a prophecy, and if those persons who consider themselves Christians believe the man Jesus Christ to be the fulfillment of that prophecy, could we not assume that there were kings of all nations at the manger? Could we not assume that maybe they were of three different races?"

Irene started to speak, but Zack Wright cut her off. (In the studio, he simply turned down the dial for the phone feed, as he often did when he didn't want to be interrupted.)

"If whoever this so-called artist is really wanted to be politically correct," Zack stated, "he would have taken the wise men out of the yard altogether. They weren't there at the stable. They found Jesus years later. So why are we willing to accept certain parts of the story and ignore others? I'll tell you why…"

Molly had stepped back behind the counter. There was no one ordering. They were all sitting and listening. No one was even moving. She looked out the window and from the far corner across the street she saw Deputy Danny Royce heading toward the shop. "Oh, my dear God."

From the speaker in the ceiling Zack Wright said, "The same reason we don't let kids color pictures of Christopher Columbus anymore. When I was a kid we colored pictures of Columbus and put them on the bulletin board, with a banner overhead that said 'Discovered America.' Now the politically correct police, who are obviously more effective than Summer Park's finest, have taken that away. Everyone who is listening to this broadcast has grown up singing 'We Three Kings' in church and Sunday school. Any adult knows there may have been more, there could have been one of each race, but we respect the tradition—and we give ourselves credit to know the truth, or what could be the truth, without having political correctness shoved down our throats."

Several people in the shop actually applauded this comment. Molly was praying that Deputy Royce would spot a jaywalker and divert his course, but he did not.

At the exact moment that Zack Wright said, "This is WKHJ. We'll be right back," Deputy Danny Royce entered the coffee shop.

❄ ❄ ❄

Poison stood behind the counter of "Book 'Em, Danno." From here, he couldn't see the churchyard, but he saw more and more people heading in that direction. The door opened and Ms. Szuch, his English teacher, came in. "Hey, Poison," she said.

Poison briefly had that look of "Don't teachers live in the school?" He shook it off and said "Hey."

Poison really liked Ms. Szuch's English class. Ms. Szuch loved Shakespeare and Dr. Seuss. The last day of school before Christmas break, she read. During the year, she would read great battle speeches from Richard III out of a giant leather-bound *Complete Works of William Shakespeare* while waving in the air a plastic lightsaber.

"I've lost my copy of *The Grinch*," his teacher said. "I thought maybe I could get one here before they disappear."

Poison said, "I'll check and see if we have one." He disappeared into the back of the store to avoid actually making eye contact with the teacher who had recently removed him from the chest of another student.

He returned with a copy in his hand, to find Ms. Szuch talking with his dad.

Snake said, "Poison, your teacher just mentioned you had a problem at school."

Rhonda, the office manager for the Summer Park Police Department, was sharing her recipe for oyster dressing with her friend Midge, when she suddenly said, "I have to go," and hung up. Before the receiver hit the phone, she said "Sheriff—you need to come out here. Now."

Sheriff Forbes was on his feet. He did not run. He'd found in emergency situations that, if he made himself stay calm, others around him had a tendency to do the same. He walked out into the lobby of the station as Danny Royce escorted through the door, and handcuffed, Jack Lambert's brother Jimmy.

Forbes inhaled deeply and exhaled though his nose. Rhonda had learned that, when Forbes was desperately trying to control himself, he often breathed this way. She never told him that his nose whistled. (She'd once told Midge that Sheriff Forbes didn't need a siren.)

"What's the problem, Deputy?" Forbes said. His tone was completely relaxed.

"Creating a public nuisance," Danny Royce said, "and threatening a police officer."

"I never did," Jimmy Lambert said. He had trouble saying this, because the Deputy had laid him over the reception desk, and his face was currently flat against the simulated wood-grain top. This was not the first time Jimmy Lambert had seen the sheriff's office desk this close up, nor would it be the last time. However, this time Sheriff Forbes stepped in. "What happened?"

As Jimmy's story went, he had watched the deputy come into the coffee shop and speak with Molly behind the counter. Jimmy had decided to fake snoring, which had made several people in the shop laugh. When Deputy Royce ignored him, Jimmy made the noise louder. This got him a glare. As the deputy turned to leave, Jimmy had sneezed into his hand while saying a profanity that compared the deputy to a lower part of the body. Deputy Royce had turned. Jimmy had then made the mistake of standing up and saying, "Bring it on, Sleepy."

The telling of this story took a good twenty minutes. All the while, Sheriff Forbes never moved an inch—not even to scratch his ear, which was itching like crazy. When everything had been said, and everyone was breathing a little easier, Forbes uncuffed Jimmy Lambert and said, "Making a threatening gesture to a police officer can get you in serious trouble, Jimmy."

This was a well-practiced speech. Sheriff Forbes had said it, in some form or another, several times. "Drinking in the back of a pickup can get you into serious trouble, Jimmy. Showing your butt to the mayor can get you in serious trouble, Jimmy. Climbing the water tower with a can of spray paint can get you into serious trouble, Jimmy." Sheriff Forbes knew this was just one more in a line of speeches that would go ignored. So far, the only actual damage Jimmy had done was to the water tower, on which he had misspelled some four-letter words.

"Go home, Jimmy," Forbes said. Jimmy walked past Danny Royce, who was the color of a poinsettia. Although, if Danny Royce thought about it, it was Rhonda who sneezed into her hand while saying one of the words that Jimmy had misspelled on the water tower.

Danny Royce looked at Forbes in disbelief. "How can..."

"Not here," Forbes said.

"You just..."

"Danny," the sheriff warned, "not here." Forbes turned and walked into his office. The deputy followed him. Forbes stood by the door and waited for Danny to sit down and then gently closed it. "Do you need a break?" He said quietly.

"What?" Danny asked.

"Do you need to take some time off? Do you need a vacation until the Nativity thing is done?"

"No," Danny said flatly.

"Everybody gets stressed, Danny. You've been taking this personally."

"Zack Wright is making it personal."

"Zack Wright is a windbag," Forbes said. "If he makes our job harder, then our job is harder. You're a police officer."

"Do you remember when that carried respect?" Danny said.

Forbes was quiet. "I'd have to think about it."

Deputy Danny Royce stood up. "I'm fine. I don't need a break. I'll take my vacation in February just like always."

Forbes nodded. "I'd recommend getting away. Go find a beach."

Deputy Royce nodded and said, "That would be nice."

❄ ❄ ❄

Later that evening, in the last row of the balcony of the Summer Park Community Church, Rev. Tumbler sat with his back to the wall, staring at the large stained glass window. The window showed an abstract design that, in the right light, could be seen as a man hanging on a cross. Though the cross was not distinctly sculpted into the glass, the face of the crucified man was. Tumbler said to the face, "You want to tell me what's going on? What is it I'm supposed to learn from this? Is this my cue? Do you want me to go? Is this my nudge out the door?" Tumbler waited as he often did, hoping by some chance that there might be some audible voice like that of James Earl Jones to say, "Okay, here's the deal." There was nothing but silence in the air. He looked at the newspaper in his hand. The Summer Park Gazette bore a headline that said "Wise Men Return. Holy Family Missing."

"Sounds like a kidnapping," Tumbler said, to no one in particular.

Chapter 13

There are those people in the world who like to figure out the magic trick. They see David Copperfield on television and spend the next few days trying to figure out how he switched places with that woman who was tied inside that bag inside that box. There are those who will go to the restaurants that feature strolling magicians, and hope they'll come over to the table, and try to screw up the card trick. There are those who like magic and who appreciate the artistry, and who can suspend disbelief long enough to be entertained for a few minutes by a sleight-of-hand artist or a performer with shoulder pads in his straitjacket, and there are those who know it's all an act and just can't keep themselves from telling everyone else the obvious.

Both of these kinds of people stood around the bright yellow crime scene tape that surrounded the churchyard. The king who kneeled at the empty manger held a wooden box in his hands. If you looked close enough, you could see that it wasn't really wood, it was part of the fiberglass statue. If you looked close enough, you could see just a trace of the line where the new face had been put onto the kneeling king whose head had once been empty enough to play home to a family of church mice. If you looked close enough, you could see that the jewels in the crown were not really sparkling at all—they had been painted to look as if they were sparkling. There were those who bent over as close as they could, and who then smirked and said, "See, it isn't a miracle."

There were others who walked past and wondered how the church kept the velvet robes the kings wore from getting ruined in the snow. There were others who, when a cold breeze blew through wondered why the kings' hair didn't blow like everyone else's. There were those who drove by and thought, "Oh, I guess Summer Park is doing a live Nativity this year." Some had even gone so far as to cross the crime scene tape and brush the snow from the shoulders and crowns of the kings, they looked so cold.

Betty Filmore studied the figures from all sides of the tape. Betty came to church three days a week. She was one of those indispensable volunteers who had given her life to her church after her husband died seventeen years ago. Betty sharpened pew pencils, organized the refrigerator, stuffed envelopes, served cookies, made punch, and sat in the same spot in the same pew every single Sunday. She was also the one who knew the church better than anyone else, and who would quietly inform those who were not as "informed" as she was as to what was expected of them if they were going to attend "her" church. Reverend Tumbler once asked her if these were God's expectations or hers. She responded by cutting her offering in half for a year and serving on only seven committees and not ten. When she began to get the idea that no one missed her input all that much, she decided to let bygones be bygones and came back.

Betty Filmore had painted the statues herself more than 30 years ago, and she was getting tired of this sort of disrespect. Tradition had a place. She looked at the figures and became hot enough to melt snow.

"Dey's beautiful, isn't dey," a voice said next to her.

"Excuse me?" Betty turned and saw a dark woman next to her. The woman had her head wrapped in a scarf that had a thousand different colors and patterns.

"I said dey's beautiful," Iza said.

"I think they're horrible." Betty said.

Iza looked at her and said, "You keep scowling like dat and you face is gonna freeze dat way in dis weather."

Betty looked at this woman she didn't know, and decided this person with the island accent obviously wasn't from around here and hadn't yet picked up on American etiquette. She pulled her coat closer around her and walked away.

A man on the other side of Iza watched Betty Filmore leave. "Christmas spirit," he said.

"Da baby Jesus is part of a crime scene," Iza said with irony.

The man said, "I remember it the other way. I'm not knocking the paint job, but...why can't they look like they're supposed to?"

Iza asked, "You mean like they're really supposed to, or like they did in the Sunday School books?"

"Nothing wrong with tradition. What are they going to do next? Change the hymn to..." The man then started to sing: "Good Christian Non-Gender-Specific People, rejoice, with heart and soul and voice..."

A woman a few feet away said, "You got that off of Zack Wright."

"Wright is right," the man said.

"If they catch the people that are doing this, they'll probably make them paint it back the way it was," the second woman said.

"If they catch the people who are doing this, they'll string them up," the man said.

Iza stood quietly and stared at the figures. The tallest of the kings reminded her of someone. She was having trouble remembering whom. Then she thought maybe it wasn't the face that caused the memory but the artwork. Maybe she had seen this style or this artist's work before. She remembered a boy from her art teaching days who'd used to make statues of angels. Then she remembered she had just seen the boy recently, at her Thanksgiving table. Iza dropped her bag of groceries in the snow.

❄ ❄ ❄

Doreen tried to find a station that wasn't playing Christmas music. The location of the town (down in the valley) and the time of year made it nearly impossible. Every Christmas tune seemed to hold a memory of her father. He would sing "Chestnuts Roasting on an Open Fire" whenever they drove through the town looking at Christmas lights. He would sing "Jingle Bells" whenever they went down the hill on a sled together.

She punched the "seek" button three times. Three out of the four available stations were playing holiday classics. The only one that was not was WKHJ, and they were running "The Best of The Zack Wright Show"—pre-recorded highlights from the week's arguments.

"Why the shepherds first? That's what I want to know," a caller was saying. "And I was surprised when one of the wise men didn't come back as a woman."

Zack Wright asked, "You think that could happen?"

"Obviously this person is trying to make the whole thing more politically correct. The liberals would love to think there was a queen there along with the three kings."

"We're asking the wrong questions—or at least asking them too soon," Zack Wright said. "Why isn't the church making a bigger deal about this? Why didn't the person who took the statues go to the church and say they wanted to do this? Is this some sort of plea to get some of the federally funded so-called-'art' money to make this a bigger exposition? Is there some local artist begging for bucks? Let me tell you, folks...this is just the kind of thing the government would waste your money on. These idiots who get our tax money to write words on cows and call it poetry," Zack Wright chuckled. "This is lunacy—let's take another call. Hello, you're on the Zack Wright show.

"Hi, Zack. Thanks for taking my call."

"You're welcome."

"How do we know this is a local person doing this? If this is an artist or somebody gunning for funding, wouldn't it make sense that it's someone from out of town?"

"I agree with you up to a point." Zack said. "I think it could be someone from out of town. We have to look at the fact that Summer Park is basically a quite small community. So if this was an outside job, what are the chances that it's not an artist at all, but one of the liberal groups working with the liberal media to stir something up?"

Doreen pushed the "off" button as she pulled her mother's Volvo into Poison's driveway. She was going to stay only a minute, she told herself. She had to get back to town and pick up her mother, who was doing some shopping. She was going to call Poison a jerk for keeping things from her. She was going to tell him that he was a lunatic. She was going tell him how mad she was, and then she was going to leave.

She walked to the side of the garage. The heater on the inside had fogged the window. She saw movement, and carefully pushed the door open.

Poison was in his shirtsleeves. His iPod was playing loud enough that he didn't hear her come in. He was painting the hand of Joseph.

For a moment she forgot why she was there.

Joseph was nearly complete. The hand that Poison was working on was clutching a wooden staff. His knuckles were white, as if anyone who got too close would feel the blunt end of a wooden cudgel swung by a carpenter.

Finally he looked up and said, "HEY." He said it loud, and then realized he was yelling, and pulled the earpieces out of his ears. "Hey," he said again, quieter this time.

She asked, "Am I interrupting?"

"No. I was just…"

"You lied to me."

"What?"

"You lied to me. You were in a fight."

"It wasn't a fight. Jack Lambert just—"

"You were in a fight with Jack Lambert and you didn't tell me?"

"It was just a little thing. Ms. Szuch ended it before it got started."

"So you lied to me."

"I didn't lie," Poison said. "It wasn't that big a deal. I didn't want you to get upset."

"Stop trying to protect me. Can't you just let me in a little?"

"How 'in' do you want to be? I already made you an accessory to a crime. Have you been listening to the radio? Have you seen the papers lately?"

"Yeah, you look really upset about it."

"I'm scared out of my mind."

"Then let me help."

"We've been through this already, I'm not going to…"

Doreen didn't wait for him to finish the sentence. She spun around and went out the door.

A voice behind him said, "That would be your cue to go after her." Poison turned and saw Bez-A-Lel standing there.

"Stay here," Poison said. "I need to talk to you." He turned to grab his jacket.

"Leave it," the angel said. "You'll make more points if you go without it."

Outside, Doreen had almost reached her mother's car when Poison came up behind her.

"Doreen," he said.

She turned and saw him in his T-shirt. It had been hot in the garage. He was sweating. "You're going to catch cold."

"What am I supposed to do? I need to finish this and not hurt anyone. They're going to have a 24-hour guard on the church, you just watch." She looked at the ground. Poison asked, "Are you mad because I didn't tell you about the fight, or are you mad because I told you I'd do this myself?"

"This was sort of our thing," Doreen said. "I

thought it would be just us." In truth, Doreen had already been memorizing details so she could tell her grandchildren someday about the time their grandfather stole a Nativity and put it back.

Poison shivered and breathed out a long stream of steam. "I need your help. "I can't get this done," Poison said. "I'm sorry. Will you please help me?"

She looked at him as he started to shiver. "You're going to catch cold." She said. She kissed his cheek and said, "I have to go pick up my mother. I'll see if I can come back later."

❋　❋　❋

Harry Vaughn had never been to Reverend Tumbler's house, not since before Tumbler had moved in with his family. Harry had volunteered to be on the committee that evaluated whether or not a new parish house was needed. Harry knew, of course, that a new house was not needed: that a paint job and a good scrubbing would be just fine. Harry was on the evaluation team, not the clean-up crew. Harry had also been there when the preacher moved in. Harry was a businessman. He wasn't being nosy. He knew eventually Reverend Tumbler would ask for a raise, and Harry wanted to know how the Reverend and his wife were accustomed to living. The house was plenty big and they were still a young couple. The parish would be a great place to raise a family. Now the preacher was in that big house all by himself, and Harry thought it might be time for the committee to ask the preacher to move to a smaller place. But all that was for another visit. This one was a little more official.

Reverend Tumbler opened the door. "Harry?" he said. Tumbler flicked on the porch light.

"Sorry to bother you at home, Reverend," Harry said.

"Come in."

Harry stepped through the door. He saw the preacher was wearing a college sweatshirt and a pair of jeans. On his feet he had big red hand-knitted socks that looked incredibly warm. Harry thought about it for a moment. He had never seen his pastor's feet before. It was strange somehow.

"Can I get you something?" Tumbler asked. "There's some cocoa on the stove. Real stuff, not a powder mix."

"No, that's okay, Reverend."

"I've got the big marshmallows. I'm out of the little ones. The big ones are better in hot cocoa anyway."

"I'm fine," Harry said. He didn't know if the Reverend was purposely trying to make him uncomfortable, or whether he was just feeling out of his element. In the church he was in charge. This was the Pastor's home. He had very little power here, which was something the Reverend was very aware of.

"We need to talk about the Nativity situation."

"I thought we decided to wait and see what happens," Tumbler said. "We were going to wait and see if the pieces came back on their own." He laughed a little. He liked the sound of it.

"The newspaper is full of opinion letters, and Zack Wright is talking about nothing else. We don't need this kind of publicity."

"People are talking about Christmas like it's a religious holiday," Tumbler said. "I'm not hearing a lot of talk about toys and video games and Santa. I like hearing folks talk about the baby Jesus."

"They're talking about racism," Harry said. "And we're in the middle of it."

"What are you suggesting?"

"Twenty-four hour surveillance. We find out what it would cost, and we have the police stake the place out. Then we arrest the person or persons responsible and prosecute them to the fullest extent of the law."

"On what charge?"

"Theft."

"They put the statues back."

"Criminal trespassing then."

"I think we're jumping the gun, Harry. Let's wait a few days and see if Mary, Joseph, and the kid come back."

"Pastor," Harry started, "you know I try to stay out of the way you run the church."

Tumbler nodded, but both men knew it was a lie—and each was aware the other knew it was a lie.

"But the board has the final decision. The board grants you power, but on larger issues they vote, and you have to go along."

"I don't have to go along—and one of the votes is mine." Tumbler didn't like to be "schooled" in his own home. "So, what does the board say?" the preacher asked, as he sipped his cocoa.

"The board has already met for December. But I'm going to call an emergency meeting."

"If you do that, I have to be there. That's in the church charter."

"I knew that," Harry said. The truth was that he hadn't known. He had hoped he could call the meeting without an opposing opinion. "I'll let you know when it's going to be."

"I appreciate that, Harry. Sure you won't have some cocoa?"

Harry shook his head and stood. "This is wrong, Reverend. We can't just let someone do this to our church."

Tumbler stood as well. "The only thing that has happened so far, Harry, is that some talented artist has made our antique Nativity look a lot better than it did without our permission. I still say we wait."

Harry held out his hand. "I'll let you know when the board meeting is."

Tumbler shook his hand and let Harry show himself out. When the door had closed, he sat back down in the chair and put his feet up on the coffee table. He stared into the fireplace and softly sang to himself: "'Tis the season to be jolly, / Fa la la la la la la la la."

By complete coincidence, Doreen was humming the same song as she came into the kitchen for a glass of milk.

"Oh, good," Iza said. "Now I don't have to call you to come down."

"I was just going to get some milk and then go back up and study," Doreen said. She was already inching toward the door.

Iza was standing by the stove stirring a pan of hot chocolate. "I make de best cocoa in de world," Iza said. "You used to tell me dat when you was little."

"It's true,' Doreen said. "But I have this history test and…"

"You and me," Iza said, stirring, "we not had much of a chance to sit and just talk-talk lately."

"Mom, I really need to…"

"I bet hot cocoa and gingerbread cookies still taste good together," Iza said, ignoring the way her daughter was trying to get out of the room. "You get de cups and de napkins and de mini-marshmallows, and I get de cookies."

Doreen knew she wasn't going anywhere, so she did as her mother told her to do and sat down. Iza poured hot cocoa into the cups, and Doreen added the little white cubes. "So," Doreen asked nervously, "What do you want to talk about?"

"I want to talk about dat artist you call 'Angel Boy.'"

Chapter 14

Harlan Durst had never made anyone pay to use the dolly. He called it a hand truck, himself, but most people coming into the hardware store called it a dolly—so he didn't argue. A financial consultant had once told him how much money he could make a year if he rented the hand trucks out by the day. Harlan Durst was convinced that he made that much back in return business by loaning it out for free. Durst's Hardware had done business like that for twenty-five years, and no one had ever stolen a hand truck yet.

When Poison had gone to see Mr. Durst about borrowing the hand truck to help his dad move boxes of books into the storeroom, Harlan Durst never gave it a second thought. Poison's only worry was that if his dad actually did go to Durst's Hardware to borrow the dolly, he'd suspect something was up.

Poison played the scene in his head with all the

honesty he could muster. "Mr. Durst, I want to borrow the hand truck to move several life-sized statues of the Nativity…nah, he'd never buy it."

Poison drove through the night in his father's
book van. He was more than a little surprised that
no one had reported seeing the van from "Book
'Em Danno" on the street after midnight. He was
alone. Well, not really alone. He saw Joseph in his
rear view mirror scowling at him. In the barely-
there light, Joseph seemed very peeved. "What?"
Poison asked him. He expected no response, and
got none. Doreen was profoundly grounded, and
no doubt her father was sitting guard.

Poison adjusted the mirror down, so that he was
looking into the face of Jesus' adoptive father. A
moment later, Poison passed a car on the road:
when its headlights briefly lit the back seat, Poison
saw Mary's face in his mirror. She seemed to be asking, "How could you? All that precious child wanted to do was help." Poison wanted this to be over.

The dolly from Durst's Hardware had made
moving the two statues much easier. It was still
hard to load them into the van unaided, especially
since he was trying so hard not to make a sound.
The angel statue and the baby Jesus statue sat in the
family garage. He had three days until Christmas,
and if all went well he would deliver them to the
church on Christmas Eve. His plan was to go to the
service, and then sneak out and put the final two
statues in place, so that when folks left the church
they would see the completed scene. Everyone
would say "Awwwwwwwww," and Reverend

Tumbler would have a Christmas miracle to remember. He had to get these two in place by himself. If he was quiet and quick, he could do it.

＊　＊　＊

Danny Royce had parked the cruiser near the building. He had left the station light on and pulled the mini-blind closed. Next, he took the clock off the wall and pulled it out of the plastic casing. He cut a shape out of a piece of cardboard and attached it to the second hand. Placing this on his filing cabinet and taking the shade off the lamp, he popped the battery back in. From outside on the street it looked as though a shape would pass by the window every sixty seconds. It would only be obvious to someone who stood outside and timed it. For anyone else, it would just look as though Deputy Danny Royce was working late.

＊　＊　＊

That is exactly how it looked to Poison, who drove past the police station four times. After satisfying himself that the deputy was busy, he rolled through town one last time, looking for witnesses and giving Deputy Royce a chance to finish up. Poison slowed the van, turned into the church parking lot, and drove around to the back. Any passerby would never see the van—Poison hoped it was dark enough that no one could see him if he stayed close to the building.

❄   ❄   ❄

Danny Royce sat in the Reverend Tumbler's office with the light out. He could clearly see the front yard of the church, and was confident that no one outside could see him. He had a thermos full of Molly's strongest coffee. "Papa Bear or Cave Bear or something like that," he'd told her. She'd filled it up, and now Danny Royce was living his very first stake-out. The coffee was wretched, but he had drunk so much that he was vibrating. He stared out the window at the remaining statues. The kneeling wise man looked almost silly there presenting his gift to an empty manger.

"Get used to that, Your Highness. Give him everything you got—and eventually you'll figure out that he's not there."

Danny Royce took another hit from his coffee mug. His left leg was bouncing up and down so fast that he had to put his other hand on it to quiet it. He felt a little strange being in the minister's office without the minister's permission. Danny Royce had let himself into a few offices over the years: the mayor's office, for one, when there was the rumor going around about drugs. He'd also scoped out Sheriff Forbes' office, for no other reason than that he wanted to see if he could do it without his boss noticing. The sheriff did notice—but he didn't tell Danny.

Danny did, though, have permission to be here. Harry Vaughn had given him a key. So, technically, he did have permission from the governing body of the church—just not from the person whose office it was. Still, there was something about being in the office of a man of God. On top of the filing cabinet was a plastic figure of Jesus that the youth minister had given Reverend Tumbler. In the dim light, it looked downright creepy.

Danny Royce took another hit of his coffee and waited.

Poison slowly pulled Joseph's feet out of the van and set them carefully down on the wet blacktop. He had wrapped the base of the statue in an old blanket and fastened it with duct tape. With the feet set securely on the ground, he guided the base of the dolly underneath. He stood the figure up straight, and then wrapped the two belts around the statue. When Poison walked around to start pushing, he realized that he had strapped Joseph in so that Joseph was facing him.

Poison took a minute to admire his own work. He had always thought history had given Joseph a raw deal. Most of the great Nativity artwork showed only Mary and the baby. In fact, a lot of the worst artwork also showed only Mary and the baby. The designer of this particular Nativity had done the next worst thing—not going to any great lengths to make Joseph all that different from the shepherds. Poison had stared into that blank face for a good twenty minutes before he had begun to paint. With the brush and some highlights, Poison had been able to make Joseph's hair look curly. His beard was now longer and fuller than those of the wise men. Now, standing here in the church parking lot at two in the morning with only a streetlight for illumination, Poison noticed in his Joseph a strange similarity to Tuba, the truck driver who had come to visit him the first time he saw an angel. Poison tilted the dolly backward and rested Joseph's head on his shoulder. The plaster was cold, but the feeling was still strange. Poison resisted the urge to reach up, pat Joseph on the head, and tell him it was going to be okay.

❄ ❄ ❄

Deputy Danny Royce had just returned from the fastest bathroom trip of his life. He did a quick head-count and found the same number of figures on the front lawn and took his seat again. He felt like a real cop. He felt calm and in control—so calm and in control that he didn't jump and run when he saw the man with the hand truck walk right past him. In the dark he could see the figure was a man. He watched as the man set the statue down carefully and carefully ripped the yellow tape that surrounded the yard.

"Destruction of police property," Danny said to himself. He had been collecting a list of charges he would press whenever he caught the perpetrator. Or perpetrators? Maybe there was more than one of them. He had to have driven in from somewhere. Was he alone? The figure pushed a dolly through the wet grass. There was enough snow to leave a trail. Deputy Royce didn't remember seeing such a track before. Maybe they didn't use it the first time. Maybe the first time he had help and this time he was alone. Danny's first thought was to wait and see if the figure came back with the other three statues. Then he heard Zack Wright's voice in his head. The voice said "incompetent" and "joke" and "inept." Danny picked up the phone on Reverend Tumbler's desk and dialed the Sheriff's home number. The answer came from a groggy voice that was trying to sound as if it was in control. "Hello."

"Sheriff, I got 'em."

"Danny?"

"I'm at the church and I'm watching the perpetrator put the Joseph statue in place.

"How many are there?"

"One that I can see."

"Don't do anything."

"What do you mean? He could get away."

"I'm on my way." The sheriff hung up.

Danny watched as the figure outside adjusted the spot where Joseph would stand. "He could get away," Danny told himself. The word "bungling" in Zack Wright's voice passed through his mind again; he stood up and headed for the door. The last thing he did before he went out the front door of the church was to make sure the safety was off on his pistol.

He moved out the door and down the steps. The snow that was left on the ground was wet and soft, not hard and crunchy. Danny did a sidestep around the building until he was at the edge of the front yard. He pressed his back to the brick and peeked around the corner. The figure was still trying to get the statue into the right place. The figure had his back to him. Deputy Danny Royce was as surprised as anybody at how quickly and quietly he moved. As he got closer, he could make out the black leather jacket and the blue jeans. The figure was squatting down, pulling the base of the statue toward himself. Deputy Royce stood three feet behind the man. The deputy put one hand on the butt of the pistol as the figure stood up and turned around.

❊ ❊ ❊

As much as Bez-A-Lel enjoyed humanity and the earth and all that came with it, he rarely used his human form when he prayed. When he spoke to the Creator, he was who he was. There was no "human suit," as Gabriel used to call it, between him and his Maker.

He made his rounds as he always did. Snake (known to Bez-A-Lel as Edgar) and Brenda Davenport slept in the middle of the bed. It was a sleeping habit they had picked up when they had been traveling the highways on a motorcycle. One sleeping bag was easier to carry than two—and if they simply stayed close together with their feet straight, they could both fit in one bag. The sides of the bed had gone virtually unused throughout their marriage, except if they were fighting about something—but even then, they usually wound up anyway rolling toward the middle, where a large dent had formed over the years.

Lifting himself through the roof, he floated the three blocks to Doreen's home. Doreen slept in the center of her queen-size bed. The covers were smooth and unwrinkled. Doreen slept on her back with the covers pulled up under her armpits. "Like a letter sliding into an envelope," Bez-a-Lel thought.

Passing quickly through the master bedroom, Bez-A-Lel saw Doreen's mother sleeping alone and clutching a pillow. Dropping through the floor into the living room, Bez-a-Lel stood beside the La-Z-Boy and watched Ted Hudson as he listened to a Miles Davis LP. He seemed restless and unable to relax. Bez-A-Lel put a hand on Ted's shoulder and felt "the peace" leave his own form and enter Ted's. Ted settled down and was almost instantly asleep. He would wake up again in twenty minutes when the record had finished, and wander off to bed, but would not remember in the morning how he got there.

At the home of the Reverend Tumbler, Bez-a-Lel found the minister sitting on the roof. He had searched the house for the minister, "feeling" that the man was there, but unable to find him. Finally spotting the old man through the window, Bez-A-Lel sat down next to him unobserved. Tumbler was wearing his boots and heavy coat. The minister sat and stared at the sky. It was clear, cloudless, and full of more stars than most people are used to seeing on any given night. Bez-A-Lel didn't know how long the minister had been out there, but the cold wasn't bothering him. The minister folded his hands and brought them to his face, pressing his nose to his thumbs.

"Father," he said, and then he began to weep. Being an angel, Bez-A-Lel was not permitted to intrude on prayers. He placed a hand on Tumbler's shoulder, and tried to give the man some peace, but it did not come.

Behind them in the bedroom, the telephone rang. It was one of those sharp piercing rings that seemed to happen only in the wee hours of the night. Of course, Bez-A-Lel knew immediately who it was, and what it was about. Tumbler turned and looked through the window of his house and the flashing red light on the headset of his phone. "That," he said, "cannot be good." He said it to no one in particular—which was just as well, because the angel had gone.

Bez-a-Lel spotted the police cruiser as it moved down the old county road toward town. The angel dropped through the ceiling of the car and studied the sheriff's face. There was determination but not tension. The sheriff held a cellphone to his ear and was repeating "Come on, Rev. Pick it up." Bez-a-Lel left the sheriff where he was, and sped off toward the church.

❄ ❄ ❄

Other than the whole "seeing angels" thing, Poison had led a fairly normal life—as normal as life can be for a person whose parents are former bikers and whose name comes from an Eighties rock band. He had pretty much respected his parents all his life, he mostly did well in school, he worked in his parents' store, he had friends, he had a girlfriend, he had the admiration of most of his teachers and he went to church.... well, sometimes. He had stared down a few bullies on the playground and had been in two fights. Well, three if you count the one with Jack Lambert the other day—but that had been over fairly quickly, and he hadn't been himself.

When he stood up from positioning Joseph's feet, and turned around, he found himself looking into the face of Deputy Sheriff Danny Royce. Poison gave a startled "Ahhhhhhhhhhhh" which, he would remember proudly later, didn't sound like a little girl's.

Deputy Royce's "angry cop" look softened to one of surprise. "You're that kid in the diner."

Poison did not move.

"Who else is here?" the officer asked.

"Just me."

"How did you manage to pull this off by yourself?" Royce was skeptical.

"By alienating my girlfriend, screwing up my GPA, and completely ignoring my parents' Christmas present," Poison said.

Deputy Royce was silent for a moment, then said. "You have a car someplace?"

"In the parking lot." As Poison turned to face the direction of the parking lot, he moved his hand for the first time since turning around. As he did he saw the deputy reach for his gun and bring it up so it was leveled at Poison's face. The deputy said. "Did I give you permission to move?"

"I wasn't running. I thought you wanted to go to the van."

The pistol did not move, but Poison could see the muscles in the deputy's jaw tighten. "I'm not moving."

The deputy asked, "Do you have a weapon on you or in the vehicle?"

"I'm a kid," Poison told him. "It's my mother's minivan." He saw the way the deputy was looking at him, and immediately decided this was not the place for sarcasm. He said. "No, officer."

Poison was suddenly aware of a presence behind the deputy. Bez-A-Lel appeared briefly in his natural state, and then as a glowing version of his human suit.

Bez-A-Lel had thought the "glow" was a nice touch and would put any fears to rest. With both hands, Bez-A-Lel made "slow up" motion and mouthed the words "Be cool." Poison took a deep breath.

Bez-A-Lel put his hands on the shoulders of the deputy. He felt such tension and anger that his hands nearly hurt. There was more there than was caused by the current situation. The anger and stress were built up on the officer's soul like a scar. It was no wonder he hadn't done anything when the angel touched him.

From off to the side all three of them heard the calm voice of Sheriff Forbes: "Danny. Put it away." Everything about the sheriff said he was in control of himself. His tone and his body language all said "calm." Bez-A-Lel could see the sheriff's heart beating; it gave his tension away.

Deputy Royce did not move.

Forbes said, "Deputy. You were given an order."

With a military precision, or at least the precision he had seen on cop shows, Danny Royce holstered his weapon. Poison started to breathe again. So did the sheriff. Bez-A-Lel did not breathe in the first place, but even he felt better once the gun was put away. The sheriff approached the other two slowly. "Is this our thief?"

Royce nodded. "I caught him putting the Joseph statue back."

"How'd you catch him?"

"I staked out the minister's office."

"Good work," the sheriff said.

"Thank you."

During this entire conversation, Deputy Royce had not once stopped looking at Poison. Poison could see the deputy's eyes darting back and forth between his face and his hands. Poison thought that the deputy had much too much caffeine in his system, but he wasn't going to say a word about it.

"He says he has a van in the parking lot," Danny said.

The sheriff looked at Poison. "Your folks own the bookstore, don't they?"

"Yes, sir," Poison said. He was looking past

Deputy Royce's shoulder at the angel—who was still giving him "stay calm" signs and gave him the thumbs up on the "sir."

"Is anything in the van?" the sheriff asked.

"I told the deputy I'm not armed, sir."

Sheriff Forbes covered a smile with his hand. "I meant statues, son."

Poison said, "The statue of Mary is in the van."

"And the other two, the Jesus and the angel?"

"They're in my parents' garage."

"I'm guessing your parents don't know you're here."

"Yes, sir," Poison said, feeling comfortable enough to look at the Sheriff for the first time.

"Is anybody else involved?"

"Nobody else knows I'm here, sir." Poison was fully aware that it was not an answer to the question. So was Bez-A-Lel, who first looked at him quizzically, but then nodded.

The sheriff said, "We're going to go to the parking lot now, and then we'll take you home. Okay?"

Poison's stomach felt like the first drop on the really tall roller coaster that his youth group had gone to in Ohio last year. "Yes, sir."

"You're not going to try anything, are you, son?"

"No, sir."

The sheriff turned to go and Deputy Royce motioned for Poison to follow him. The small train of people walked back down the sidewalk to the parking lot. When the reached the van, the sheriff said, "Open it."

Poison did. Mary was on the inside, kneeling. Her hands were in the air—normally a gesture of awe at the sight of the holy Christ child, but now she seemed to be saying, "Oh, you got caught. I knew you would."

Reverend Tumbler's car pulled into the parking lot. Poison looked around for the angel, but he had gone. Tumbler got out of the car, his coat still on over his sweats and hockey jersey. He stood and looked at the freshly painted Mary in the back of the "Book 'Em Danno" van. After a while, he said: "That's nice work. You really have a touch."

"Thank you," Poison said.

Tumbler looked back at the figure. So did Poison. Her features seemed to have softened— Poison guessed it was from the Rev. Tumbler's headlights.

"What I want to know," Tumbler said, "is why you didn't come and ask. Why didn't you come and see me first?"

The sheriff and the deputy and the minister all looked at Poison.

"It was a surprise," Poison said.

"For?" the Sheriff asked.

"For Reverend Tumbler," Poison said. "The waitress at the coffee shop said how much he hated this time of year, and we thought we could do something that would make him feel better."

Although the two police officers were aware that Poison had said "we," the Rev. Tumbler had not caught it. Neither did Poison. The deputy made a puzzled face as if he was going to ask about it but the sheriff waved him off.

"Okay," the sheriff said, "the Reverend and I are going to take Mary back to her place, and then we're going to wake your parents. Deputy Royce will stay here with you—" the sheriff raised his eyes to look at Deputy Royce, and said in a tone loaded with meaning, "—and he won't touch his gun."

Danny Royce glared upward—embarrassed to be corrected by his boss in front of a minister and a thief—but said nothing. He glared at Poison after the minister and the sheriff had unloaded the statue from the van.

"I borrowed Mr. Durst's hand truck," Poison said. "It's still out front."

"That's not doing us a lot of good now," the sheriff said, grunting under the awkward load.

When the sheriff and the minister were on the sidewalk and out of earshot, Deputy Royce leaned in close to Poison's face. Poison could smell the coffee on his breath. Royce said—as if it were all one word—"Igotcha."

❊   ❊   ❊

The doorbell rang five times before Brenda shook her husband awake.

"Snake, someone's at the door."

"Wha?" Snake said groggily.

"Someone's at the door," she said again. "This time there was worry in her voice. "Go see who it is before they wake Poison."

Snake threw his feet over the edge of the bed. He wore black sweats with the word "Pittsburgh" down one leg and "Steelers" down the other. He lumbered toward the bedroom door and clutched the railing as he made his way down the stairs. He rubbed his eyes and flipped the switch on the porch. He tried to peer through the peephole, but his eyes were still asleep and he couldn't focus, so he simply opened the door.

On his porch were two police officers and a minister. Snake thought it sounded like the beginning of a joke he'd heard before, but then he saw his own son in the middle of the trio. Snake leaned his head against the door jamb. "Oh, God."

"Mr. Davenport," the sheriff said, "is this your son?"

"For the moment," Snake growled.

"Mr. Davenport, I'm sorry to wake you, but it appears your son is the one behind the incident involving the stolen pieces from the Nativity at Reverend Tumbler's church."

"He put them back, didn't he?" Snake said. Poison at first took this as a positive sign that his father would not be mad. His father had had a number of run-ins with the police during his biker days, and knew how to talk his way out of a lot of situations. This was an automatic reflex that kicked in, and that—Poison would later find out—had nothing to do with his father's anger level.

"What's going on?" Brenda appeared at the top of the stairs in her fuzzy bathrobe. She looked down at the porch and suddenly gasped. "Oh, my God, Poison? What's wrong?"

Snake turned to talk in his wife's direction. "Apparently our son is the Nativity thief." When he turned to say this, the two cops and the minister caught just a glimpse of the snake tattoo that wound its way down the father's back. It was old, and some of the details had faded, but it was still impressive.

Poison's mother said, "Oh, my God," and sat down on the top step.

"Mr. Davenport," the sheriff said, "I'd like permission to go into your garage. The boy says the remaining statues are there, and we'd like to take them with us. You don't have to let me in, but I can get a warrant."

"That's not necessary," Snake said. "Let me get my coat and shoes." He looked down at his son and closed the door. The sheriff turned to walk away. Danny Royce grabbed the back of Poison's collar and pulled him in the direction of the garage.

Snake appeared a few moments later with a leather jacket pulled on. They could still see his bare chest beneath it. His feet were covered by tennis shoes, which he had not bothered to tie.

He came toward the garage and looked at his son. "I take it this means that there is no Christmas present." Although sarcastic, the comment was not meant for humor. Poison would later learn that sarcasm, too, had nothing to do with his father's anger level. Snake opened the door and flipped on the lights of the garage. Poison led the group over to the area where he had set up his "studio."

Everyone stared. Poison's eyes widened. He turned around and said, "They're gone."

"What?" Almost everyone said it at the same time, except for Danny Royce.

"They're gone," Poison said. "The angel and the baby. They were here. They were almost done. I swear they were here when I left." He turned back and looked at the empty space where the statues had been. He thought that if he looked away and then turned back again, they might reappear. They didn't. He began searching under the tarps, as if maybe they had moved. They had not. The angel and the baby Jesus were no longer in the Davenports' garage.

Chapter 15

When Snake had said, "We'll talk about this tomorrow," Poison really thought that he meant sometime after 10:00. After all, it was about 3:30 when he finally crawled into bed. "We'll talk about this in the morning" was the last thing he remembered hearing from his father.

His bedroom light went on just a few hours later. His father said, "Get up. I need some help in the store today."

Poison was groggy only for a moment, and then he remembered the depth of the trouble he was in. He got out of bed and was showered and downstairs in ten minutes, which was a record for him. His mother was there. She was sitting at the table holding, but not drinking, a cup of coffee. Poison was going to say something about the time, but it dawned on him that neither of his parents had been to bed since he'd come home. He decided at this moment that it would be much better if he said absolutely nothing for as long as possible.

Snake pulled two travel mugs down from the top shelf of the cupboard. There were more than thirty there: mugs with various sports teams, gas stations—and the complete collection of Bragger's Bagels mugs, which changed every year. Snake filled both with coffee and asked, "You take cream and sugar?"

"Cream," Poison said. Actually, he liked chocolate milk—but there was none in the refrigerator, and he thought special requests were a bad idea this morning. His dad poured cream into his son's cup and covered it. He opened the cupboard and tossed a pack of unfrosted cinnamon Pop-Tarts at his son. Poison caught it and placed it in his jacket pocket. Snake bent over and kissed his wife and went out the door. Poison stood there a moment before he realized it was time to go and he was supposed to follow. He picked up the coffee mug (a Bragger's Bagels Series 8) and looked at his mother. She managed a smile, but it wasn't a happy one. He followed his father out the door.

It was a long drive in the dark. Poison caught himself sitting as close to the door as possible. He forced himself to slide over and actually sit in the passenger seat.

He looked around the van. It felt different to him, even though he had been driving it not that long ago.

Snake pulled a pack of Pop-Tarts from his own pocket and opened it with his teeth while he drove with one hand. He pushed one pastry out of the foil like a frozen push-pop and chewed silently. Poison was not hungry. He sipped his coffee in the heavy silence.

Eventually his father said, "I'm waiting for you to start this conversation. I'm at a loss. You know I've had run-ins with the police and I know what some of them can be like. I think I know what Deputy Royce can be like. But I do know that Sheriff Forbes is a good man, and so is Reverend Tumbler. Your mother and I have been up since you got home, and we haven't been able to come up with anything to do about this. So I'm waiting for you to start this conversation. It doesn't have to be now, but it should be soon. Okay?"

Poison sipped his coffee again. He said, "It's big. It's bigger than you think, and I don't know how to say it all."

"You have to start," his father said. "I won't interrupt. I've never known you to do anything without a reason. So, for right now, I'll just listen. I reserve the right as a parent to yell later, but right now...I'll listen."

Poison debated in his own mind. Everyone he had told before was now in serious danger of getting in as much trouble as he was. He could argue that he somehow forced Doreen into it or that he coerced her somehow. However, this was as deep trouble as he had ever been in. Furthermore, he was losing his father's respect.

"Do you remember when Tuba died?" Poison asked.

Snake was surprised. He hadn't expected the conversation to start this way. He was prepared for a talk about gangs or drugs or drinking, but this took him off guard. "Yeah," he said, "but I didn't think you did."

"Do you remember when I told you about how the angel brought Tuba to my room?"

"Yeah."

"Did you believe me?"

Snake was silent. He looked over at his son, who was just barely illumined by the morning light.

"You mean, did I believe that somehow an angel of God brought my best friend to your room, so that you could get a hug goodbye?"

"Yeah," Poison said. "Not in a dream and not in a figurative way, but an actual, very much real, angel of God and a dead truck driver right there in my room."

"Yes," Snake said. "I believed you. I don't know how it happened and I certainly couldn't come up with a logical explanation. For a while I thought it was a coincidence that you had a dream about Tuba on the same night he died, but then I decided I wasn't in a position to judge what was and what wasn't possible."

"I never saw Tuba again," Poison said. He took a deep breath. "But the angel has been coming back off and on for the last twelve years."

Snake sat quietly. This definitely was not what he expected.

"He's never spoken until recently," Poison said. "He just hung out and waved sometimes. Last month he showed up and told me I had a job to do, but that I had to figure out what it was and then do

206 | Steven L. Case

it. I figured I was supposed to help Reverend
Tumbler get back his spirit of Christmas, so I decided that I was going to re-paint the Nativity set. I
didn't think it was something I was supposed to get
permission for. I wanted it to seem like a miracle. I
took the pieces, I put them back, and I got caught,
and I swear to you I have no idea what happened
to the missing pieces." Poison took a deep breath.
He had spilled nearly everything. He felt so much
better, but he could see the crease deepening in his
father's forehead. "Not what you thought it was
going to be?"

"No," said Snake. "Not at all."

"So now you get to decide whether or not your
son is mentally ill or if he really talks to angels."

"Why didn't you say something to your mother
and me?"

"First, I didn't think you'd believe me— and second, the angel said that anybody I told might get
hurt."

"Did you tell anybody else?"

"I don't want to answer that right now."

Snake nodded. He continued to drive until they
reached the store. As they got out, he said, "I need
the new shelves in the back room put together.
They're all kits in boxes—most of it you can do on
your own. If you need an extra pair of hands, come
and get me."

Snake was fumbling with the keys. He realized
after a moment it was because his hand was shaking.

"Dad?"

"Yeah?"

"If you decide you believe me, then you can't tell Mom. The angel said that everybody who knows might get hurt."

"I know," he said. "I need to think."

Poison followed his dad into the store. He set his coffee mug down and took off his coat. He walked to the back room and started to open up the boxes containing the shelves. He read the instructions. It didn't look too complicated.

❅   ❅   ❅

Zack Wright sat in his office. He had his Bible open and was looking for passages that he could use on the air. He leaned back in his chair so he could better shout out the doorway. "Kelly?"

"Yeah," Kelly said. She was the receptionist, and even though the station had purchased an intercom system last year, no one used it. The station was small enough to let anyone in it simply shout and be heard. The control booth was soundproof, so anything short of a hurricane couldn't be heard by the DJ or the listening public. Doris Brant was on the air playing light rock and reading the news. She did not even look up.

"You go to church, right?"

"You already asked me that."

"Is there any place else in the book that talks about the birth of Jesus?"

"You already asked me that, too. I gave you everything I knew."

"How come the Book of John doesn't have the Christmas story?"

"You'll have to ask him that."

"Thank you," Zack Wright said. "You've been a wonderful help."

"No problem," Kelly said.

The phone rang. Kelly, the receptionist, picked up and said, "WKHJ, home of the Zack Wright Show, can I help you?" She said this in fluent receptionist-speak: a tone that was both pleasant and business-like, a tone that said "I'm really glad you called—but mess with me, and I'll kill you."

Kelly listened. She said, "Just a moment. I'll see if he's in."

Zack Wright knew it was for him. He was the "he" who was in the building right now. He was fully prepared to tell Kelly to take a message.

"Zack," Kelly called out.

"Yes?" he shouted.

"Are you in for a Robert Schober?"

Zack Wright stopped what he was doing and was silent. He called back to her, "Put it through." He picked up the receiver and stood. He leaned out as far as he could, and pushed the door closed with his foot. He punched the button and said "Zack Wright."

The voice on the other end said, "Zack Wright? Bob Schober, WHYK. Is this a bad time, or can you talk?"

Zack Wright sat down at his desk and said, "This is a good time. What can I do for you?"

Schober said, "I see your numbers have been going up."

"Better each rating period," Zack said. He actually had very little idea of how the rating system worked, but he knew his numbers were good. He could fake the conversation if he had to.

"Your résumé has come across my desk."

"Oh, I sent that some time ago. I'm really quite happy here now. I've just been offered a raise." The two lies flowed effortlessly off Zack's tongue.

"Well, WHYK would like to make you very happy," Schober said.

Zack Wright held the receiver away from his head and silently pumped the air twice and mouthed the words "YES! YES!" to no one in particular. He held the receiver back to his ear and said, "I'm listening."

❄   ❄   ❄

The sheriff tapped lightly on the glass of "Book 'Em, Danno."

Snake came to the door and opened it. "Your wife said the two of you were here. I need to speak with both of you, together."

Snake stepped back. The sheriff stepped inside and removed his hat.

The sheriff looked at Snake. In another time, they might have faced off under other circumstances. "You sleep?" the sheriff asked.

"No," Snake said. "You?"

"A little. I've been on the phone since about six."

"I'll get Poison," Snake said. He disappeared into the back room. The Sheriff looked around the room. He saw a series of romance novels on the top shelf. For just a moment, his heart lightened a little. He remembered how much his wife liked those books. He remembered a Christmas where he had wrapped up a hundred books, one by one, and left them all over the house. She had left a long time ago—and still, when he saw something she would have liked, he briefly thought about buying it, and then remembered that it would do no good.

Snake came back into the room followed by Poison. The sheriff noted how much their body languages were alike. The boy definitely looked like his mother, but he stood like his father and the two of them crossed their arms at the same time.

Sheriff Forbes put on his calm voice. "Son, if it were me I'd just want to get the pieces back and be done with the whole matter. The Reverend Tumbler feels the same way. He said he understands what you were after, and he appreciates it."

Poison and his father nodded. The sheriff noticed again how similar they were. The "But" was hanging in the air for all of them.

"But," he said, "the Reverend is not in charge of the church. Technically, he's an employee of the church, and a board runs the church. Harry Vaughn has called me and said they will press charges if the pieces aren't returned."

"What charges?" Snake asked.

"Vandalism. Trespassing. Theft. Out after curfew. Destruction of private property," the sheriff said. "All little things, I grant you, but this Zack Wright guy has made this into a federal case. The record will follow you around—could affect college entrance, but I'm most concerned with what the public perception is going to do to the business."

Poison looked at the floor. He had let his father in on the secret, and already he was getting hurt.

"If I were you, Mr. Davenport," the sheriff said. "I'd close for inventory today. Word is already out. It will most likely be in the paper, and I have no doubt that Zack Wright will make it a topic of conversation today."

Snake nodded. "Not a problem,"—but Poison could hear in his father's voice that it was most definitely a problem. Snake asked. "How long do we have?"

"Mr. Vaughn wants the pieces outside the church on Christmas morning, or they'll press charges. So, twelve-oh-one on the twenty-fifth. That's the deadline."

"I don't know where they are," Poison said. "I told you."

"Somebody else has them, then," the sheriff said. "You said that no one else was involved, but I think you and I are both aware that that answer is not exactly true. You need to find the pieces, or I can pretty much guarantee you'll be eating Christmas dinner in a cell or the sheriff's office. I have nothing else to do on Christmas, and I'd hate to see you there. There will be no one to set bail until the twenty-sixth."

Poison took a deep breath and repeated, "I don't know where they are."

"That's not what matters," the sheriff said. "What matters is where the pieces are on Christmas morning."

❄   ❄   ❄

Ted Hudson was running late. In spite of being up late and having no memory of going to bed, he felt like he'd had the best night's sleep he'd had in weeks. The phone rang and he expected his daughter or his wife to get it. When it kept ringing, he walked down the stairs carrying his black shoes. His tie was undone and he didn't smell any coffee brewing. This was a bad sign, on a morning that had started out pretty good.

"Hello?"

"Ted, it's Harry Vaughn."

"Hi, Harry. What's up?" Ted checked his watch and couldn't figure out why Harry Vaughn would be calling him so early.

"Thought I'd let you know before I left the house—you know that kid you asked me about, the one your daughter is dating?"

"Yeah," Ted said, "What happened? Another fight?" He was trying to talk on the phone while putting ground coffee into the coffee maker.

"Nah," Harry said—he was almost giggling. "The kid is the Nativity thief."

"What?" Ted said. He dropped the scoop of coffee on the floor.

"Deputy Royce caught him last night."

"Is he in jail?"

"No, the sheriff has let the little twerp go. He says he lost two of the pieces and doesn't know where they are."

"He lost them," Ted repeated.

"Yeah, can you believe it? Anyway the board has decided that if the little punk doesn't cough them up, we're going to press charges. I thought you'd like to know."

"Yeah. Thanks, Harry," Ted Hudson said. He stood there and listened to Harry break the connection. He stood there with the cordless receiver in his hand and coffee grounds on his socks. "Doreen!" he called.

Ted put the phone back in the holder on his way by. "Doreen! You know that boy that I've been telling you is no good for you? Do you know?" He opened her daughter's bedroom door, and found the room empty.

"Doreen?" he called, louder.

He waited a moment and then said, "Iza?" There was no answer from his wife, either.

❊   ❊   ❊

"What I want to know most is…" Sheriff Forbes paused. "…why you had your weapon out."

Danny Royce had expected a pat on the back. At the very least, he was hoping for another "Good job."

He had not slept, but he felt better than he had

in a long time. He felt like a cop. He understood why the sheriff had let the kid go home. Not something he would have done, had he been sheriff—but the kid posed no flight risk, and the sheriff had lost his edge since his wife had passed away. Danny thought he would have at least taught the kid a lesson and let him spend one night in the cell. That's what the deputy would have done. Now, he was defending himself.

"I had no idea if he was armed, and at the time I had no idea that it was a kid," Deputy Royce said.

"When you saw he was a kid, you didn't holster your weapon."

"He could have been armed."

"Did you have your weapon out when you approached him?"

"Yes."

"Did you tell him you had the weapon out?"

"No."

"Did he make any threatening motion toward you whatsoever?"

"He could have been armed."

"Danny," the sheriff said, "you've been itching to cause hurt to somebody. First it was the Lambert kid, and now this."

"They're not pressing charges. He's going to get a slap on the wrist."

"You were aiming your gun at a seventeen-year-old unarmed kid."

"The pieces are back."

"Not all of them," the sheriff said.

"But they will be."

"Deputy, I want you to take the day off. Tomorrow is Christmas. I'll take the entire shift. Stay at home. Celebrate the day. Ease up."

"I'm fine."

"It wasn't a request, Danny. It was an order."

Danny Royce held his position for about a second and a half. The sheriff saw his body begin to shake, and then he turned on his heel and went out the door, shoving it open so hard that the wreath fell off the front side, rolled down the steps, and settled in a puddle of slush.

Half an hour later, Rhonda tapped on the door of the Sheriff's office. This was as busy a day as they had in a long time. "Sheriff?"

The Sheriff was pinching the bridge of his nose and waiting for the aspirin he had swallowed to take effect. "What is it, Rhonda?" He said. His voice was tired and weary.

"There are a woman and young lady here who say that they were involved in the taking of the statues. They say they took them. They painted them. And that the young man was bravely trying to cover for them."

The sheriff looked up at her. She made an "I dunno" sign and left his doorway.

Sheriff Forbes walked his quiet-man walk out into the lobby of the Summer Park Sheriff's Office. He saw two women standing there, obviously mother and daughter. The mother was obviously "not from around here." She had her hair wrapped in a brightly colored scarf. She stood tall and proud. The younger one next to her looked as though she just might bolt out the door if he said "Boo."

The sheriff said, "You took the statues."

The woman said, "Dis is correct. We took de statues. We paint dem. We put dem back. De boy, he had not'ing to do wit' dis. He was 'posed to wait for us to help wit' dem. All de boy do is drive de van."

"So the boy who is the artist didn't do any of it."

"My name is Iza Hudson." Iza said. "You don' remember me, but we met when you come to de school a few years back to talk to de children about drugs. I'm de art teacher."

"I remember," Forbes said. "And your accomplice is?"

"Dis is my daughter, and we take full responsibility."

"Then I take it you know where the last two statues went," the sheriff asked.

"There's two missing?" Doreen said. She didn't seem to notice that she had created a slight hole in her mother's confession, but Iza did. Her gaze faltered from the sheriff's just a bit. Then she stood, waiting.

"You gonna arrest us, or what?" Iza asked.

Sheriff Forbes pinched the bridge of his nose and wished he had an aspirin or a baseball bat. One or the other would take care of his headache.

Everybody who listened to Zack Wright on the

morning of the 24th heard something different. Most couldn't put their finger on what it was, but there was a difference. Those who had been listening for a long time heard it almost at once. From the moment he said, "Good morning. This is the Zack Wright Show. I'm Zack Wright," they could hear a renewed sense of purpose. They could hear a new energy. In his voice, they could hear the taste for blood. He was pulling no punches.

"For those of you who don't pick up your paper and don't turn on your radio except to listen to this broadcast, I appreciate it. I really do. But that means you come to this table uninformed....and we must be informed if we are to understand the day's news. What is new today? By now, most of you know that the Nativity Thief has been caught— and, as it turns out, is one of Summer Park's own. It was not an outside group, as may have been theorized by some. It was, in fact, one individual. One young individual. One seventeen-year-old individual who pulled off the crime of the century here in Summer Park, with nothing more than a borrowed hand truck.

"But there is more...this microphone has learned that not all of the pieces have been recovered...that a warrantless, but willing, search of the alleged perpetrator's residence revealed a lack of two pieces. The angel and the baby Jesus are missing and unaccounted for.

"Questions still unanswered: Why did the alleged thief take the items and put them back? Where are the missing pieces? Is it possible that

someone else was involved? What is the real reason
behind the painting of the pieces to be more, shall
we say it again, politically correct? We will discuss
these—and other questions regarding one teenager's plans to steal Christmas—after this commercial
break."

Noticeably absent from Zack Wright's opening
teaser was any mention of the Summer Park Police
Department. In fact, in the three hours that Zack
Wright would be on the air, he would not mention
the SPPD other than to say it was a Summer Park
police officer that had apprehended the individual.
This was part of the deal Danny Royce had cut
when he called Zack Wright about ten minutes
before he went on the air.

Danny Royce was sitting in his car listening to
the program. He knew that Zack Wright had a lot
more information than had been disclosed so far.
Some of it he was keeping to use later in the program to get folks to stay tuned in. Some of it he was
sitting on until the station's lawyers decided how
much they could actually say. Danny Royce knew
what was coming, and he was smiling.

❄   ❄   ❄

At three o'clock that afternoon, Nicole
Hamilton walked into Richard Bennigan's office
with a smile on her face. She sat down without
being invited, and looked at him, still smiling. He
looked up at her, and after a beat he said. "What?"

She tossed a newspaper on his desk. The head-

line read, "Teen Artist Arrested in Nativity Theft."
She said, "Jesus and the angel are missing."

He picked up the paper. "Excuse me?"

"Remember Summer Park?"

He nodded.

"They caught the thief. It's a kid, and now the last two pieces are missing. If the kid doesn't produce them in 24 hours, they press charges."

"Are you kidding me?"

"Nope. The whole town is buzzing. Half the town wants to string the kid up."

"And?" Richard prodded. He was trying not to think about her smile.

"And—" she said—"we send a crew out there."

"On Christmas Eve?"

"Yes," she said. "And we either film the kid bringing back the missing Jesus, or we film him getting arrested. Either way, it's good video."

Richard sat back in his chair and stared at her. "Who produces?"

"I will," she declared. "Give me one on-camera talent and a camera person."

Richard said. "I'll give you a camera man. Give me footage with sound, and we'll do a voiceover at the noon report on Christmas Day."

"Deal."

She was out of the office and around the corner—and had made sure she was completely out of his eyesight—when she began to dance.

❇   ❇   ❇

Rev. Tumbler was sitting in his office as Harry Vaughn paced back and forth across the twenty-year-old carpet. Tumbler said, "Harry, you cannot put a seventeen-year-old kid in jail on Christmas Day."

Harry Vaughn said, "Reverend, the board was unanimous in its decision."

"You pushed it though, Harry."

"You weren't there."

"I wasn't invited."

"Reverend, our church was robbed."

"The town is watching, Harry. The Pittsburgh Press is sending a reporter. Harry, KADK is sending someone with a camera crew."

Harry looked up at the minister. Tumbler immediately regretted bringing it up.

"Where did you hear this?" Harry asked.

"They called me for a quote."

"And what did you say?"

"Why do you need to know?"

"Because," Harry said, exasperated, "it's my job as head of the board to look after how the church is being perceived in the community."

"Harry—if this makes KADK news, it will go all over the world. We will be seen as the church that threw a child in jail on Christmas Day."

"We'll be seen as a church that gave a last chance to some flaming liberal artist who was trying to rip out every tradition we hold sacred at this time of year," Harry countered.

"You practiced that, didn't you?"

"What?"

"You planned that out and practiced saying it, in case they called you for a quote. You planned that quote, didn't you?"

"Reverend Tumbler," Harry said, "this church has not taken a stand on any issue in years. We have become irrelevant—and if some punk kid with a paintbrush has to do community service, then so be it."

"Harry, if we press charges against that kid, we become the Pharisees. We become the self-righteous religious people that care more about religion than people."

"So tradition means nothing. Is that what you're saying?"

Tumbler leaned forward at his desk. "I'm saying that if Jesus and the angel don't show up, and you press charges against that kid for doing what he thought was a wonderful thing...you can find another minister to deliver the Christmas morning sermon."

Tumbler said this as seriously as he could. He was fully prepared to back it up.

He looked at Harry Vaughn's face. He was sure, if just for a moment, that Harry Vaughn smiled. Harry said, "The board has already discussed that too."

❄   ❄   ❄

Doreen knocked on the glass of the bookshop door. She had to do it twice, because her mittens were too thick to make any noise. Poison came to the door and smiled. She didn't smile back. He knew she was still angry at him but she was standing there with a cardboard cup carrier and two coffees from Hylander's. He opened the door for her.

"Where's your dad?" she asked.

"Went to see Reverend Tumbler."

"Then they really are going to press charges?"

"It's not Reverend Tumbler's doing," he said as he closed the door behind her. "Apparently he has no say in the matter. The board is doing this." She handed him the cup of coffee. "Thanks."

"You should have waited," she said quietly.

"I was trying to get it over with," Poison explained. "I keep screwing up. I told my dad about the angels."

"You did what?"

"I had to. I didn't know what else to do."

"What did he say?"

"Nothing yet. I think that's why he went to see Reverend Tumbler—either to get spiritual advice, or to tell him that I'm crazy."

"What about the Jesus and the angel?"

Poison hesitated. "I was hoping you had them."

"Why would I have them?"

"Because you were mad at me. I thought that maybe you took them because you wanted to be in on it. Nobody else knew about them."

"My mother knew."

"How did your mother know?"

"She was your art teacher. She came to me and said she thought it was you because she always liked your work."

Poison didn't know whether to be honored or angry. "What did your mother say?"

Doreen looked at him.

"Doreen, what did your mother do?"

"My mother believes in angels." She didn't say it very loudly.

"You didn't—"

"I told her it was a God thing." Doreen tried to smile.

"You told your mother."

"Yes."

"About the angels."

"Yes."

"And that I took the statues."

"Yes."

"And your mother decided to…"

"Confess."

"Confess what?"

"Confess that she took the statues and that you just drove the van and let us use your garage."

"Oh, my God."

Doreen said, "It really seemed like a good idea. It made sense when she told me."

"And you didn't stop her?"

Doreen paused. "I went with her."

"Oh, my God."

"What?" she said. "My mother will give this some credibility. Now it's just not two teenagers stealing stuff."

"It was supposed to be just one teenager stealing stuff."

"Well, now it's not."

"You didn't have to do that," Poison said. "You could have just kept your mouth shut, and no one would have ever known. What do you think this will look like to your father? What do you think this will do to your college applications?"

He turned and laid his forehead on the pile of paperbacks on the counter. He bumped his head against them several times before taking the entire pile and throwing it across the room.

"I did it because it's the truth, and because I love you," she said. "The sheriff sent us away. You were caught and you denied that any one else was involved, so he sent us away. If they decide to press charges, then he'll come and get all of us."

"I have to find the pieces," Poison said. The fact that she had actually said "I love you" still had not registered in his head.

"I don't know what to do to help you," she said. She wished with all her heart that she knew where Jesus and the angel were.

❋　❋　❋

Ted Hudson was awake and sitting in his chair when his wife and daughter came home. Iza gave her daughter a gentle push toward the stairs. Doreen, taking the hint, went upstairs quickly without saying anything to her father.

Ted Hudson was not even pretending to read Wright is Right. He was just sitting there, waiting for his family to return.

Iza hung her coat in the closet and walked into

the living room. She walked toward her husband and gently swatted his feet. He moved them from the footstool so that she could sit down.

She pulled it closer, till their knees were touching.

"Did I ever tell you about my grandmommy?" she asked.

Ted Hudson looked up at his wife. He was so hurt and so angry that he was shaking. Still he managed to say, calmly, "I met her, didn't I?"

Iza smiled. "Yes, you did. You met her de one time when you came to my island for de first time. She was de old, old lady who t'ought you were dere to collect de rent. Remember she scream at you and t'row an apple at your head."

Ted Hudson smiled in spite of himself. He remembered. "Crazy old broad," he said.

Iza smiled too. "Yes. Crazy. You best be ready 'cause I hear dat's hereditary."

Ted Hudson stared at his wife. He wanted to say, "You're already there." He didn't, but the look he gave his wife said it to her just as plainly.

"When I was a little girl, my momma and daddy would send me to live wit' my grandmommy during de summertime. Not many tourists in de summer, so t'ings are slow. My grandmommy had a vegetable garden, and she would send me out to pick de tomatoes. I would bring dem all inside in my apron and she would sort dem on de counter. Anyt'ing that was smaller dan a baseball would go into a bucket under de sink. Anyt'ing dat was bigger would go into de pot for making sauce or putting in canning jars. I was a little girl and I never t'ink to ask why she puttin' de tomatoes in de bucket. One day, I was supposed to be takin' a nap in her big bed and it starts to rain outside. I look out de window to see de rain and I see my grandmommy. She out in de rain getting soak and wet, and she got dat bucket wit' her. She would take to the side yard where my granddaddy had put up a stone wall a long, long time ago. One by one, she would pick up a tomato out of dat bucket and den t'row it as hard as she could at dat wall. She do it over and over. She don' care dat she gettin' wet. She screamin' in a rage at de top of her lungs, she beat her fists on her legs and den shake 'em up at de clouds. And den when de bucket is empty, she fall down on her knees and she cry, cry, cry."

Ted Hudson listened. He loved when his wife told stories. He loved her voice. It was like a song to him sometimes.

"My grandmommy come back in de house and I was terrified of her. I hid under de covers and I don' want her to see that I see what she did out by de wall. She was such a nice lady. She love me so much and I love her but every time it rain I t'ink of her out dere throwing old tomatoes at de wall."

Ted Hudson asked quietly, "What was she raging at?"

Iza put a hand on her husband's knee. "Life," she said. "Grandmommy wanted so much more. She wanted to leave the island. She wanted to be something other dan de wife of a drunk. She want to be famous. She want to sing. Mostly she want to go far far away. But she never did. She grow up. She get married. She have babies. She make her husband dinner and do his laundry and pick him up outta de puddle when he fall down. She do these t'ings because dat's what she was supposed to do. She was told dat's all she was ever supposed to be."

Ted Hudson started to speak and then stopped himself.

"Your baby girl love you so much. She love you more dan she love any man. But you got dis picture in your brain of what she supposed to be and every day you put another big rock in dat stone wall. She gonna have to go over it and not come back or she gonna spend her life throwing t'ings at it."

"What am I supposed to do?" Ted Hudson said.

"I dunno," Iza said. "I don't have answers. I just tell de stories."

She patted his leg and said, "You fall asleep in dat chair again and I'm gonna bust you on de head. You come to bed." She took his hand and she led him to their bed. She lay in the crook of his am and listened to his heart. He lay listening to her breathing for more than an hour, and eventually fell asleep too.

Chapter 16

Poison rode in the backseat of the van. Snake drove. Brenda sat in the passenger seat, willing herself not to cry. In all their years of marriage, Snake had never kept a secret from his wife, but had not yet said anything about the angels to Poison's mother. They had agreed to get through this holiday and then fill her in on everything. He wasn't taking this one day at a time anymore. He was taking this minute by minute. In spite of his fears for his son, he hadn't felt this alive in a long time.

Poison lay down on the seat and watched the streetlights pass by overhead. He had done this as a boy. He would count the lights—and, more often than not, was asleep before he got to a hundred. He was not sleepy now. He lost interest in counting somewhere around 46.

"You used to ride like that when you were little," Brenda said. She was remembering the baby who looked up at her from the sidecar of the motorcycle. He would stare at her, and then each time a light would "whoosh" by, he would turn his head to see what it was and then look back at her as if to ask, "What the hell was that?" This face was repeated over and over as they drove across the country. She never got tired of it.

"Poison, if you're protecting someone…"

"I'm not," he said, a little too loudly. "I already told you I'm not. I don't know where the angel and the Jesus went."

She turned back around to look out the windshield. "My son has never been arrested before," she said. "I don't know how I'm supposed to act."

"I'm turning myself in," Poison said, sitting up. "It's not going to be an episode of Cops or anything like that. No one is going to force me to the ground and slap the cuffs on me. I'm not resisting." In the dim light of the dashboard, he could see by his mother's face that the image of his surrender had done nothing to calm her nerves.

They had decided not to go to Christmas Eve services as they had gone every year since they had moved to Summer Park. Brenda was in favor of the show-'em-nothing-is-wrong approach, but both Poison and Snake felt that their presence in the congregation might take away from what everyone was supposed to be there for. Snake had already decided he would never set foot in that church again, but that was an argument to be had at a later time—some time *after* his son had been released from the one-cell security facility in the Summer Park Police Station.

❄ ❄ ❄

Sometime around five o'clock that afternoon, the Reverend Bill Tumbler wadded his Christmas Eve sermon into a ball. As the custodian, Mr. Disbrow, pushed his cleaning cart by the door, Tumbler sent the sermon in a perfect arc and landed a clean two-pointer in the trash bag.

He got out a yellow legal pad and a fine-point Sharpie marker and nailed together a Christmas Eve sermon on the forgiveness of Christ. Using his thesaurus, he found every possible alternative word for "forgive," and he used every one.

From the pulpit that night, he directed every comment toward the back row where Harry Vaughn sat with most of his cronies on the administrative board.

Harry didn't move, didn't flinch, and didn't smile; for all intents and purposes, he was a stone. "How appropriate," Reverend Tumbler thought.

All in all, it was one of the finest, most passionate sermons he had ever preached in that church. Tumbler decided it was a good one to go out on, so if that's what it came to…so be it. In spite of his frustration, he hadn't felt this alive in a long time.

After the service, the good people of the congregation (which seemed remarkably larger than usual on this Christmas Eve) blew out their individual candles, filed stoically out of the church and stood around in the front yard.

No one left.

Everyone was waiting to see what would happen next.

The crowd that was already outside when the church ended reluctantly made room for the newcomers. Some made comments under their breath about who was there first. Everyone surrounded the yellow police tape. The light on the top of the church entrance had been redirected down into the empty nativity. Some of those in attendance had not yet seen the new statues. In the dim light no one seemed more concerned about the missing Jesus than his life-like parents.

Iza looked at the face of the Virgin Mary and started to cry. "To lose your baby that way," she thought. "You poor girl." Ted Hudson looked at Joseph and felt a strange kinship with a man who was about to have a lot of trouble raising a child who was so far out of the box that he didn't know what a box was. Ted looked around and whispered to his wife, "Where's Doreen?"

Iza did not look around. She simply whispered. "She here. She gone to find her boy." Ted Hudson did not make his sniffing sound. He turned his attention back to the man staring at the empty manger.

Reverend Tumbler watched all this from the window in his office. He tried to ignore it, the way you'd ignore an elephant in your living room. It doesn't matter how hard you try—you can't. He put on his Cleveland Browns stocking cap and his overcoat and went out to join the throng of people that had gathered in the front lawn of his church.

He saw the van from KADK and the pretty young woman who seemed to be telling the cameraman what sort of shot she wanted. The Reverend pulled his scarf a little higher around his clerical collars. He did not want to be on camera. Not tonight.

Harry Vaughn saw the van, too, and immediately went over in that direction to "make a statement on behalf of the church."

Jenny Van Dyke (a/k/a Jenny the papergirl) had performed a solo in the service. She'd sung, "Oh, Holy Night," and accompanied herself on her guitar. Apparently she had a voice like an angel. Almost as one person, members of the congregation had leaned to someone close by and whispered, "I didn't know she could sing."

Jenny was standing outside, and thought it would be appropriate to try out a new Christmas song she had finished but hadn't had the nerve to ask Rev. Tumbler to let her play during the service. She began to strum—and in a perfect voice, she sang...

The darkness is gone and the world is in light,
The baby is born on the Bethlehem night.
The people have come to see the miracle,
And the people have come to see the miracle.
It was cold and lonely in the dark cattle shed,
And the girl remembered what the angel had said.
And the people have come to see a miracle,
And the people have come to see the miracle
The carpenter took the girl as his bride.

He stood by the manger, his face full of pride,
And the people had come for a miracle,
And the people have come to see a miracle,
The light from the star illumined the sight:
This baby king born to set the world right,
To free us from hatred and fill us with love,
To bring us the truth from the God up above
Who walked on the earth and who died as man,
Come gather round, people,
and worship the Lamb.
All the people have come for a miracle,
And the people have come to see a miracle.

A van with the WKHJ logo pulled up and Zack Wright emerged from the passenger seat. At first, folks thought he was going to do some of remote live broadcast, but he stood quietly at the back of the crowd. He waved to those who recognized him. Rev. Tumbler noted that he stood just enough apart from the crowd to draw attention to himself.

Poison watched all this through the window of the darkened bookshop. He was not in a hurry.

A few people in the crowd had brought signs. One said, "John 3:16." Another said, "Jesus is not a terrorist." When Jenny had started to sing, the sign-wavers had stopped waving.

"All they need is some lighters," Snake said.

"It's not a Grateful Dead concert, Honey." Brenda put one hand on her husband's shoulder and the other on her son's back.

Snake said, "Poison, I think it's time."

Without saying a word, Poison opened the door of the bookshop and began walking toward the

Summer Park Sheriff's Office. Snake began to follow, but Poison asked, "Can I do this by myself?" Snake stepped back. Brenda was amazed at how much her son's voice suddenly reminded her of the biker who had stolen her away nearly twenty years ago. She was going to give him a list of reasons why he should have his mother along, but her husband's hand on her shoulder stopped her.

Sheriff Forbes stood on the steps of the Sheriff's Office and waited. He was watching the crowd, not expecting any trouble, but observing the crowd just the same. He had hoped the boy would be able to produce the missing statues, but that didn't seem as if it were going to happen.

As Poison crossed the street and stepped over the curb into the churchyard, Harry Vaughn spotted him. Harry nudged the man next to him, who looked. The man with Harry Vaughn pointed, and everyone turned.

Nicole Hamilton said something to the cameraman, who spun quickly and adjusted the camera. A light above the lens came on. Those who had not seen Harry Vaughn point now turned to see what the camera was seeing.

Poison took a deep breath and kept moving. Aware that all eyes were on him, he refused to look. He suddenly felt a familiar mitten on the bare hand in his pocket. He turned—Doreen was smiling at him. "You don't have to be here," he told her. "I need to do this by myself."

"I didn't ask."

"Your father—" He started.

"—doesn't know you. That's his loss. Let me go along. I was part of it—let me see it through."

He didn't answer her in words. In his jacket pocket, he clutched her hand a little tighter. He looked at Sheriff Forbes, who was still waiting for him on the steps of the police station.

From out of the crowd, Deputy Royce stepped in front of Poison and Doreen. "Are you prepared to hand over the stolen items?"

At first Poison didn't recognize the deputy out of uniform. He said, "I, uh…"

Behind them on the steps, Sheriff Forbes hung his head. "Oh, Danny," he said, and began to walk toward what he knew was a bad situation getting worse.

"Officer," Poison said, "I don't have the statues, and I don't know who does." Poison was going to offer his hands for the cuffs—but as he held out his wrists, Deputy Royce grabbed him by the front of his jacket and yanked him forward. Poison stumbled and went down. Hard. His chest hit the frozen ground and all the air went out of him. Danny Royce shoved a knee into Poison's back, pinning him down. Doreen screamed. Poison lay gasping…pleading for air that would not come. Deputy Royce pulled a set of handcuffs out of his jacket pocket.

Sheriff Forbes started to run. So did Snake. Deputy Royce rolled Poison over. Poison would have given anything to clutch his chest or tell someone that all he was doing was sucking air without releasing any.

"He can't breathe," Doreen said. Her voice was on the edge of panic. She turned and saw Snake coming. "He can't breathe!" she shouted.

Poison closed his eyes and felt a hand on his chest. His lungs suddenly filled with clean fresh air. When he opened his eyes, there was no one there but the deputy who had begun to read him his rights.

Sheriff Forbes arrived a moment before Snake and was able to hold him back from pounding on the deputy sheriff. Danny Royce lifted Poison to his feet. Poison looked over Doreen's shoulder at his mother and her parents as they came through the crowd. Behind Iza and Ted Hudson, there was a bright light. Poison and everyone around him assumed that it was from the television camera.

But then it got brighter.

The light grew intense, and soon everyone turned from where the deputy sheriff had thrown the teenage artist-thief to the front of the church-yard. The light got still brighter, and seemed to be coming from everywhere, yet from nowhere.

In the sudden brightness, people squinted and held their hands up to their faces.

Mary was the first one to move.

The hands, which Poison had so painstakingly re-created, seemed to tremble at first and then lower by themselves. It was no longer a superior paint job. It was flesh and bone. Her face slowly and cautiously turned toward the crowd.

Sheriff Forbes stared at the statue. Deep in the folds of the brown hood, the shepherd stared back at him with his son's face. He seemed to recognize his father standing there and he smiled at his amazement.

Forbes tore his eyes away, half terrified that this vision might vanish. He looked at Reverend Tumbler, who was also staring fascinated into the light. As far as the minister could see, the statue of the mother of Christ looked identical to the woman he had lost to a car accident years ago. In the hands of a now-real, live angel, his own son looked at him and made a face at him, the way he used to.

Doreen stared into the light, as each statue in the Nativity seemed to sway. The Joseph she had watched being repainted turned slowly, and smiled at her with her grandfather's face. She started to cry. Glancing away, her eyes landed on her mother who was standing in the crowd. Her mother was weeping as well.

Brenda, who had caught up to her husband in the commotion, now stood beside him—as the shepherd who looked amazingly like Tuba winked at them.

A wave of awe swept through the crowd as each person recognized grandparents, sisters, brothers, parents, and children who had been lost.

Poison, who was still disoriented from his fall and his sudden healing turned to look into the face of Bez-A-Lel. The angel hovered over the manger, holding what many would swear later was a real infant. The angel lay the child down in the straw and raised his arms. The light that enveloped the crowd grew brighter until the glare was too much and even those who didn't want to look away had to do so, or cover their eyes.

The last one to see what happened was Poison, who did not look away, and who was fairly sure that Bez-A-Lel smiled at him before the light went out.

People blinked their eyes and took their hands away from their faces. There in the middle of the yard was a completed Nativity: angel and the baby set perfectly in place—each of them painted in the same style as the others.

Zack Wright yanked a cellphone from his jacket pocket and dialed the station studio line and demanded from the intern who was working on Christmas Eve that he be put on the air immediately. The intern, who knew only how to push the "start" and "stop" buttons on the machine that played 24 solid hours of Christmas music, said she didn't know how to do that. Zack Wright began to scream, and the intern began to push buttons at random.

The applause started from somewhere in the crowd. More and more people picked it up—and soon, all those who had come to watch a young man be arrested were caught up in a moment of pure joy. A few of the calmer ones saw the theater lights hanging in the trees and pointed these out to those around them. Harry Vaughn saw them too and had no idea where they came from.

Doreen turned to Poison and said, "They think it's a show?"

Poison nodded. He had to give Bez-A-Lel credit.

Reverend Tumbler, who fully believed what he had seen was a miracle, turned to look at the single tear that was running down the face of the town's sheriff. The sheriff looked at the minister, and instantly they each knew what the other had seen.

"Danny," the sheriff said, "take the cuffs off."

Deputy Danny Royce, who had seen his own father's face and immediately dismissed it as a hallucination caused by stress, started to protest—but instead obeyed his boss. He removed the cuffs. Poison opened his arms receiving his girlfriend into them. She cried into his shoulder, and he held her close: rocking her gently back and forth. "I saw him," she whispered. "I saw him."

Poison felt a hand on his shoulder and looked to see his own dad crying. If there had been any doubt in his father's mind, it was gone now.

"Merry Christmas," his father said, and wrapped his arms around both his son and the girl who would one day be his daughter-in-law.

Poison looked out over the crowd at the statue of the angel: a statue he had not painted, but was painted nonetheless. He had studied that plaster face, but this one was different. This one was an angel, he knew.

Epilogue

In the coming days, most people who were there thought one of two things.

Some decided that the whole event was an elaborately staged production created by a very talented young man who would obviously go on to bigger and better things. They believed that the sight of long-past friends and family members was a trick of the imagination, of the kind that often happens around holidays.

There were those who saw and believed instantly, but decided that it would be best to keep the miracle to themselves rather than mention it out loud to anyone.

On Christmas morning as Snake lay in bed with his wife's head resting on his shoulder, he could tell she was awake. He asked, "Did you..."

She said "Yes," before he could finish the question. Neither of them mentioned it again—but each knew when the other was thinking about it.

✳   ✳   ✳

Nicole Hamilton and her cameraman checked the videotape in the KADK van, and found that the camera had quit working moments after the deputy sheriff had thrown the boy to the ground. She went back to the station and told her boss that the artist had returned the pieces, and that she had footage of an undercover officer abusing a suspect who was in the process of surrendering. The footage made national news. When she told her boss of the event, she tucked her hair behind her ear and Richard asked her to dinner.

✳   ✳   ✳

Deputy Sheriff Danny Royce was dismissed from his position, and took a job as a security guard at Summer Park High School. In the first year after his dismissal from the Summer Park Police Department, Security Officer Danny Royce revived a sixteen-year-old girl from an accidental overdose of pills. He also tracked down the source of the drugs, and personally escorted the individual (Jack Lambert, who had taken the pills from his brother's room) to the police station. He did not stay to chat.

✳   ✳   ✳

In the course of the investigation, Sheriff Forbes interviewed several of the teachers at Summer Park High School, and was invited by the Advanced

English teacher to a home-cooked meal. They were married six months later on Christmas Eve.

❋   ❋   ❋

Zack Wright, in his efforts to guide the intern at the studio towards putting his call live on the air, became frustrated and unleashed a stream of profanity that included all seven of George Carlin's words you can't say on the air, and some new combinations of the seven that hadn't been included in Mr. Carlin's original list. Zack Wright also made a comment that was later termed "a disparaging racial insult." The intern, whose name was Andrea, finally managed to hit the right button, and all of Zack's Wright's comments were heard on the air by everyone who was listening: including Tanya Schober, little sister to Robert Schober—who, upon hearing the story from his baby sister, immediately rescinded the job offer he had made to Zack Wright just a few days before.

❋   ❋   ❋

Poison Davenport was not arrested. Ever. For anything. He and Doreen married two years after they graduated from college.

Poison has an angel-sculpting business. Some are made for tabletop center pieces; others are more than eight feet tall. He sells them over the Internet. He has made thousands, and no two are alike. He has won several awards. Doreen teaches elementary school.

❄   ❄   ❄

Irene the waitress had been stunned to learn she was the sole beneficiary of Tuba's estate. It turned out to be a sizable sum. Irene didn't tell anyone. A few years after Tuba died, Irene had contacted a lawyer and quietly bought the diner. As the new owner, she promptly fired her boss and renamed the diner Tuba's Place. She's still there. They have really good chocolate cake.

www.ingramcontent.com/pod-product-compliance
Lightning Source LLC
Chambersburg PA
CBHW071145260626
47162CB00003B/928